Welcome to Harlequin's great new series,
created by some of our bestselling authors
from Down Under:

THE AUSTRALIANS

Twelve tales of heated romance and adventure—
guaranteed to turn your whole world upside down!

Travel to an Outback cattle station, experience the
glamour of the Gold Coast or visit the bright lights
of Sydney where you'll meet twelve engaging young
women, all feisty and all about to face their biggest
challenge yet...falling in love.

And it will take some very special women to tame
our heroes! Strong, rugged, often infuriating and
always irresistible, they're one hundred percent prime
Australian male: hard to get close to...but even
harder to forget!

The Wo___
where spirit___
Australia'___

D1649336

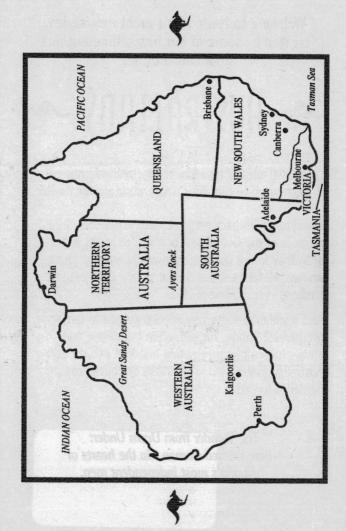

THE AUSTRALIANS

OUTBACK HEAT
Emma Darcy

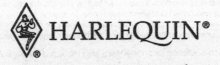

HARLEQUIN®

TORONTO • NEW YORK • LONDON
AMSTERDAM • PARIS • SYDNEY • HAMBURG
STOCKHOLM • ATHENS • TOKYO • MILAN • MADRID
PRAGUE • WARSAW • BUDAPEST • AUCKLAND

ISBN 0-373-82573-0

OUTBACK HEAT

First North American Publication 1998.

For a woman who calls fiction writing "the hardest of all activities" she's ever tried, **Emma Darcy** has certainly proved herself able to meet the challenge. The former actress, painter, architect and teacher has written more than sixty novels since 1983, and has over 60 million copies of her books in worldwide print. Ms. Darcy lives in New South Wales, Australia.

CHAPTER ONE

HEAT enveloped her like an oppressive blanket as Angie left the air-conditioned taxi and headed up Queen Street Mall to the Hilton Hotel. It was sticky, humid, enervating heat and the city was sweltering in it, typical for Brisbane in January. It would be hotter in the outback, Angie reflected. Weatherwise it would be the equivalent of jumping out of the saucepan and into the fire...if she got the job.

But she could cope with that. Angie clung to the idea she could cope with anything as long as she got Brian Slater out of her life. Committing herself to a year of working as a governess on an isolated property in the outback seemed ideal for making a clean break and forcing it to stick. No easy come-backs in that situation. She would be right out of Brian's reach, in every sense. Besides, the heat there was dry, not like this sauna sizzle on the coast.

Entering the hotel was pure bliss. She scooped the hot weight of her hair away from the back of her neck to let the cool air erase the dampness that had gathered there. The curls tended to frizz on days like this so pinning it up would have resulted in tendrils wriggling free. Better to let the shoulder-length mass hang, rather than risk an untidy appearance. First impressions were important in a job interview.

She examined her image in a mirror. No damp patches on her dress. The soft lemon colour looked fresh and cheerful, not too bright against the golden tan of her skin. It suited her, complementing her brown hair and amber eyes. The button-through style of the dress was smart, without being overly professional, the right touch, she hoped, for a governess.

Satisfied her lipstick hadn't bled and she still looked respectably turned out, Angie checked the time. Five minutes left before she was to meet the man who could give her an effective escape from the emotional mess she was in. It might be cowardly to run from it but she didn't care. She was too vulnerable to Brian's persistent pursuit of her while ever she remained in Brisbane. She needed this job. Really needed it.

The directory by the elevators listed the Atrium Room on the sixth floor. The interview was to take place in the lounge area adjacent to the restaurant. As Angie rode up to her eleven o'clock appointment, she worked hard at keeping nervous tension at bay, taking slow, deep breaths and mentally rehearsing her answers to obvious questions.

It wasn't easy to project a composed and confident front when she felt so churned up over the situation that had developed with Brian. Somehow she had to put him out of her mind, as well as out of her life. The next half hour or so was critical to winning her best opportunity to do that. She fiercely told herself to concentrate all her energy on impressing the man she'd come to meet.

Skylights above the Atrium Room provided a large pool of natural light for ferns and other tropical plants to flourish. The softly cushioned cane furniture in the lounge area was inviting, more a pleasant social venue than a business one, Angie thought, but undoubtedly intended to put the applicants at ease. She was wondering how many were to be interviewed as she scanned the occupants of the lounge; couples, groups of ladies, one lone man. The moment her gaze locked on him, Angie felt a frisson of shock.

She hadn't formed any expectations...just a man of the land, needing a governess to supervise his children's lessons from the school of the air. He emanated strength. He wore an aura of strength. He looked carved out of some hard substance that didn't belong to ordinary flesh and blood. Bred to endure, Angie thought, and she felt intimidated by the impact of a power she'd never encountered before.

He saw her, nodded an acknowledgment and rose to his feet, preparing to greet her with civilised courtesy. He wore city clothes; grey trousers, blue shirt, nothing to mark him as an outback man, but the clothes were totally irrelevant. He was impressively tall and broad-shouldered, yet with a wiry leanness that suggested he could move fast and efficiently if action was called for. There was an almost animal maleness about him that seemed to deride any form of civilisation.

Darkly tanned skin was stretched taut over strong facial bones. Although he looked too toughened by life to be called handsome, he had the kind of face that was stamped with an innate authority, compelling attention and respect. His hair was black and straight, as were his eyebrows, though they had a slightly downward slant, shadowing eyes that were surprisingly light.

Angie's pulse was fluttering wildly as she forced herself to walk toward him. She knew intuitively this man wouldn't be fooled by anything. It made her feel intensely vulnerable. Even her legs felt shaky and doubts flooded her mind. Would the preparation she'd done for this interview be enough to satisfy him? It seemed all too possible his judgment would be based on standards she knew nothing about.

* * *

Taylor Maguire absorbed the stunning impact of her as
she wove around the tables between them, her purpose-
ful approach obliterating any doubt as to her identity.

Angie Cordell… teacher…applying for the position of
governess…his mind reluctantly acknowledged the unwelcome facts even as his body reacted to a sexuality
that thumped into his heart, sent a surge of blood to his
loins and stirred urges that made him wish this meeting
was in a far different situation.

If *she* had walked into the bar last night…

He'd had his choice of a number of pick-ups—easy
sex—sex he needed to settle the fermenting frustration
of being celibate too long—yet in the end he'd recoiled
from taking it from women who'd held no real attraction
apart from the physical release they might give him.
Empty sex. He didn't really want that. He wanted…

This woman.

Such lush femininity…a cloud of shiny brown curls
bouncing around a soft, beautiful face…skin gleaming
like honey satin…an appealing freshness about her
lemon dress which somehow accentuated the sensuality
of full breasts thrusting against it, the seductive sway of
perfectly curved hips, the graceful movement of long
legs. Its line of buttons could open all of her to him…if
only she wasn't Angie Cordell applying for the impossible position of governess.

Impossible.

No way could he take her.

He struggled to resist the temptation of her, to quell
the arousal of instincts he couldn't afford to indulge, to
be the man he had to be…*in this situation.*

His eyes were blue, piercingly blue and chillingly cool.
Angie barely suppressed a shiver as she came to a halt

beside the table he'd chosen. Whatever assessment he'd made while she approached was obviously not warmly positive. Nor was he about to turn on any superficial charm. A smile would have to be won from this man. Unlike Brian, who gave them freely to everyone.

"Miss Cordell..." He offered his hand. "...Good of you to come." His voice was deep and pleasant and as strongly male as the rest of him.

"Thank you for giving me your time, Mr. Maguire," she replied, determined to hang on to an air of confidence no matter how much he rattled her.

The handclasp was brief, over before Angie could even register what his touch felt like. Cool and controlled, she thought, watching him direct the play; gesturing her to the chair opposite his, summoning a waitress, inquiring what refreshment Angie would like, efficiently disposing of the order, everything settled within the space of a minute or two, including himself.

He sat across the table from her, focusing intently on her eyes. The typed sheets of her résumé were on a clipboard, lying on the chair adjacent to his, but he didn't glance at them, probably having gleaned all the information he wanted. Angie felt he was now fitting her to the facts he'd read.

"Why do you want this job, Miss Cordell?" he asked as smoothly as a highly sharpened knife, slicing through to the key concern behind her application.

Angie rolled out her prepared answer. "I've always wondered about life in the outback. This will give me first-hand experience."

A sardonic gleam appeared in his eyes. "I don't run a tourist operation. Giralang is a working cattle station. The view is unchanging and the activities could be considered boringly repetitive."

"Not to you, Mr. Maguire," she said with certainty, sensing he would treat a gush of positive aspects from her with contempt.

"No, not to me," he agreed, his mouth curling in ironic appreciation of her counter-thrust. "I was born to it. I see it differently."

She nodded. "I'd like to see it through the eyes of those who live there."

He could hardly contest that desire, Angie thought, her spirit fired by his antagonistic approach. Why was he being so negative? Had he taken one look at her and decided she was unsuitable?

She would not give in to such a superficial judgment. It wasn't fair. If Mr. Taylor Maguire thought he could arbitrarily dismiss her from his list without a proper hearing, he could think again. She was fed up with not being listened to, having her needs dismissed as irrelevant. For a stranger to do it…this rock of a man…on top of Brian's capricious habit of ignoring what she said…

"Have you ever lived in the country, Miss Cordell?"

She could feel his prejudice and railed against it, even as she pitched her voice to appealing reason. "No. But I once knew someone whose life changed very much for the better after working for six months on an outback station. What he said about it has always stuck with me. I'd like to know for myself how it is."

Funny how she'd instantly thought of Trav Logan when she'd read about the advertisement for a governess. She'd been mad about him in her troubled teen years, drawn to the excitement of his wild reckless energy. A magistrate had given him the option of six months on an outback station or the same time in a correctional institution. Trav had chosen the wide open spaces and it had completely changed the direction of his life. He'd gone jackerooing after that, saying the city was stuffed and the real challenges were outback.

Trav…thriving on the edge of danger. Brian did the same, trading on the floor of the stock exchange. The link suddenly raised a disturbing thought. Was she compulsively attracted to men who liked living dangerously?

"The contract is for a year, Miss Cordell," Taylor Maguire reminded her with a quiet but forceful emphasis, snapping her attention back to him. "A year is a long time. Especially for a city person, used to having entertainment on tap."

He wasn't going to beat her on that rap, either. "I've never been short on commitment, Mr. Maguire. When I take on a job, I see it through."

"Very commendable. However, there is a difference between doing a job and being happy in it."

"I like children. I enjoy teaching."

"Then why give it up for what is basically a supervisory position?"

"I don't consider it would be giving it up and I'm sure your children would benefit from the expertise I can bring to extending the lessons given on school of the air."

Angie could barely contain the anger burning through her. He'd read the résumé she'd given to the employment agency. If he'd considered her overqualified for the job, why grant her an interview? He had to know she could offer more to his children than a minder, so why was he backing off? Would it do any good to confront him with his unreasonable attitude, attack rather than defend?

He was regarding her thoughtfully. Maybe she was getting through to him. It was probably best to let him pursue his own agenda first before trying more active persuasion. Angie waited for the next question, resisting the temptation to break the testing silence.

The waitress returned with their coffees, cappuccino for her, short black for him. Angie stirred in a spoonful of sugar. Taylor Maguire left his unsweetened. Not for him a ready kick of energy, not even sugar. She thought of Brian's growing cocaine habit, his excuses for it and the broken promises that trailed in its wake, and fervently wished she had never become involved with him.

The basic truth was she wanted out—out of her whole life as it currently stood—and if she didn't convince this man to take her into a different world with its own in-built support system, she would have to face up to some other kind of drastic move. Shifting house wasn't enough. Brian didn't want to accept it was over for her and sometimes she was scared he never would.

She replaced the spoon on the saucer and sat back, gesturing her readiness to continue the interview. The coffee would be too hot to drink just yet and the need to win Taylor Maguire's approval had an added urgency. A compelling urgency.

She wished his blue eyes weren't so piercing.

"You're a trained teacher with five years of classroom experience," he started again, picking up on the résumé she'd sent to the employment agency.

"That's correct."

"I imagine you earn very good money, Miss Cordell, much more than a governess."

"The cost of living in the city is high." Especially over the years of trying to fit into the trendy lifestyle favoured by Brian's social circle. Most of his friends came from wealthy backgrounds and seemed to have money to burn. She'd once thought herself lucky to be welcomed into their privileged world. She'd been blinded by the glamour of it but her eyes were wide open now. "I won't be losing, Mr. Maguire," she said with certainty.

He frowned. "You've weighed all this?"

"Yes."

Free meals, free accommodation, nothing to spend her wage on, no fashion stakes to uphold...she'd probably end up financially ahead. Not that it mattered. She was after peace of mind, not economic improvement.

She could see her lack of doubt had unsettled him, disrupting his line of argumentation. It prompted a wry little smile from her. "Some things can't be measured in money, Mr. Maguire."

"Enlighten me," he invited.

"Experience."

The sceptical gleam winked out. He returned her smile, though it was more a twitch of his mouth than an actual smile. "The cost of experience can be very dear, but I take it a smaller income is not an issue to you."

"I have no cause to quarrel with it. As I understand, from the employment agency, the salary you're offering is more than the usual for a governess."

Something dark and foreboding flickered in his eyes. "Perhaps you should have asked yourself why, Miss Cordell."

The drawled words didn't carry a threat, more a touch of self-derision, yet they stirred an unease. "I prefer information to indulging in guessing games," she said cautiously. "I'd like to hear from you what the situation entails for me."

He shrugged, visibly relaxing before answering her. "There are three children on the station who require lesson supervision. You would be used to handling many more so that wouldn't present a problem to you.''

"They're not *your* children, Mr. Maguire?"

"Only one. My son, Hamish. He's seven years old."

"Most of my teaching has been with seven-year-olds."

Another wisp of a smile with a twist. "That fact did draw my interest, Miss Cordell."

So what was turning it off? What problems did he see in her taking up the position? "Does your son have learning difficulties?" she probed.

"No. He learns whatever he wants to very quickly," he said dryly.

"A case of not wanting to?" Angie queried.

"Let's say he's become very selective in hearing what's said to him. He lost his mother last year. She was piloting a small Cessna. An engine caught fire and it crashed," he stated, his delivery matter-of-fact, strained of all emotion.

"I'm sorry," Angie murmured with sincere sympathy. "Losing a parent is always disturbing to a child."

Losing a wife was no picnic, either. Grief could bring people together or drive them apart. She couldn't see Taylor Maguire sharing his grief with anyone. He would bear it alone. Which probably meant the child had felt shut out and even more bereft of parental love and care.

"It hasn't been easy for him," he admitted. "And I doubt Hamish will welcome you. He may even perceive you as trying to take his mother's place."

"I can only assure you I would be sensitive to your son's feelings, Mr. Maguire. Given the chance, I would try everything I could to win his trust and confidence."

She meant it. It would give her a real sense of purpose, over and above the educational one. To do something meaningful, to turn something bad around, to make a caring difference to a child...for the first time she felt a positive eagerness toward the job, rather than seeing it as a personal means of escape.

"Unfortunately, Miss Cordell, others would see it the same way."

Her mind still fixed on the emotional hurt of a little boy, Angie didn't catch his father's drift. "I beg your pardon?"

"I'm a widower. You're a very attractive woman. I presume you're unattached or you wouldn't have applied for this position. Your résumé gives your age at twenty-seven, a time when most women have either formed a permanent relationship or are looking for one."

Angie was flabbergasted by the implication. "You think I'm out to catch you?" she spluttered.

He shrugged. "I'm merely telling you what you'd be walking into. We'd be living under the same roof. With others there, as well, but that won't stop the gossip. Gossip is rife in the outback, Miss Cordell. The chat radio session is prime entertainment."

"Well, firstly let me assure you I'm not a desperate female out to ensnare a man, Mr. Maguire," Angie bit out in a flare of resentment. "Not you nor anyone else. In fact you could say men are very low on my priority list at the moment."

"Then you shouldn't be moving into a man's world, Miss Cordell, because you will inevitably draw their attention."

Like Brian's? Everything within her recoiled from a repetition of what she'd been going through. "I trust I'd be under your protection." No one would pit themselves against *his* strength, she thought, hugging the sense of security it gave.

His eyes hardened. "If you stir trouble, I can't guarantee absolute protection."

It's not my fault, she wanted to cry. A desolate hopelessness swept through her as she realised why the interview was taking this course. "So that's the problem. You took one look at me and decided I'd be too much trouble."

"It's a possibility I'd be foolish to ignore," he conceded.

Frustrated by a view she couldn't disprove, Angie searched for a way around it. She shook her head. "I'm neither a flirt nor a tease, but I guess I can't expect you to take my word for it." And it was impossible to change her physical appearance. She looked at him in bleak appeal. "I hope you won't ignore what I can give."

"I am taking that into consideration, Miss Cordell," he assured her. "I felt it was only fair to warn you of matters you might not have considered."

True enough. She had thought more of getting away than what she was going to. "Thank you. I appreciate it," she forced out, momentarily wishing she was dead.

She leaned forward to pick up her cup of coffee, needing to calm herself and reassess where she was now.

In all fairness to him, the live-in situation was a tricky one, given his newly single status. He looked to be in his mid-thirties, the owner of a vast cattle station, certainly not unattractive physically. Most people would consider him "a catch." He wasn't to know she was immune to any man's appeal right now.

On the other side of the scales, it was surely natural for him to want the best for his child, which was why he'd chosen to interview her. A sympathetic teacher with absolutely no sex appeal would not have presented the potential problems he saw with her. Somehow Angie had to defuse them, diminishing the negatives and accentuating the positives.

She drank the coffee and set the cup down again. He hadn't touched his. She glanced up to find him watching her, his eyes narrowed, thoughts shielded. Had he already made up his mind or did her chance at the job still hang in the balance? Impossible to tell. She had to strike at what was most important to him.

"Would gossip worry you?" she asked. Somehow she couldn't believe it of him. Idle talk would be water off a duck's back to this man.

"The woman is usually the target. Especially a newcomer." His eyebrows rose in challenge. "Do you have a thick hide?"

"You're talking of people I don't know, whose opinion wouldn't count with me. As long as I'm fine within myself about what I'm doing, and I would be," she added with conviction, "what other people speculate about wouldn't hurt."

"Not many people achieve such self-containment, Miss Cordell," he said quietly.

You have, she thought, and wondered what had driven him inside himself. Did the outback breed such men, demanding a self-reliance that absorbed adversity and moved on past it?

"I can only tell you how it is with me," she answered, clinging to simple dignity. "I'm at a point in my life where I'm not looking to others to make something of it for me. I need time for myself."

He made no comment. He observed her keenly and she sensed his curiosity, but he chose not to pursue such a personal issue, perhaps wary of crossing the line of non-involvement.

"I am good with children," she went on. "This past

year I had a class of fifteen pupils who'd dropped behind their year's standard of learning because of various behavioural problems and physical disabilities. Most of them I was able to help make the grade, and the others at least had a happier year at school. The headmaster would confirm that appraisal if you'd like to call on him. The telephone number is in my résumé.''

He nodded. ''Is there anything else you'd like to tell me, Miss Cordell?''

He was winding up the interview. Panic fluttered through her. Had she said enough? Still his face gave nothing away. Desperate to leave him with a strong impression of her capabilities, Angie pressed one more point.

'I think I'd understand your son, Mr. Maguire. I was an only child myself. My father died when I was eight. My mother when I was fourteen. I know the sense of...of displacement...very well.''

He frowned. ''I don't believe my son feels *displaced.*''

''No?'' Wrong move! She tried to recover. ''Well, maybe you've given him a strong sense of belonging. I simply meant I'm familiar with loss.''

Which was probably why she had found it so difficult to leave Brian after two and a half years of close intimacy. The need for a loving relationship eroded common sense. It had felt good...for quite a long while. But the bad had become too bad and she hated what it did to her.

''I really want this job, Mr. Maguire,'' she blurted out, unable to stop the raw plea which had to be visible in her eyes.

''I'll keep that in mind, Miss Cordell.'' He rose to his feet, signalling the end of her time with him. ''I appreciate your presentation and the thought you've given to it.''

Cool politeness. Nothing more.

Angie's heart sank as she stood up. ''Thank you for listening to me.''

He nodded. ''I have other applicants to interview after lunch. I'll let you know my decision this evening if that's convenient to you.''

''Yes. Thank you.''

He held out his hand. No encouraging smile. No warmth in his grasp. A brief, formal leave-taking.

Yet Angie felt his eyes boring into her as she walked away and her heart pounded with a flurry of complex feelings. She wished she had his strength. She didn't want to leave him, to have to face her own life again, alone and unprotected. Her mind cried out... *Don't let me go. I need this chance.* But he didn't call after her and she forced her legs to keep walking.

This evening, he'd said. Another seven or eight hours. Then she'd know.

CHAPTER TWO

THE heat hit her again on her exit from the hotel. Angie wandered aimlessly down the mall, drained of the energy to grasp any purpose now the interview was over. A long afternoon of waiting stretched ahead of her. She had to fill it in somehow.

Best to get out of the heat, she told herself, but didn't feel like going home to an empty apartment. The two other teachers who shared it were still away on vacation, leaving her with no ready company to provide distraction. Watching the telephone would not make it ring before this evening and she doubted she could concentrate on a book.

She could treat herself to lunch somewhere, then take in a movie.

Entertainment on tap.

Angie halted, frowning, as Taylor Maguire's words sat almost accusingly in her mind. A movie would be more an escape from her thoughts than an entertainment, she argued. Especially today. But there would be no ready escapes from anything in the outback.

If she got the job.

Was she really prepared for a day-after-day sameness that could prove boring?

Yes, she answered emphatically, as long as she felt safe. And she would on Taylor Maguire's property. No one would buck his authority. She was sure of it. And she would be free of Brian. Boredom was a small price to pay for the removal of the stress he was causing her.

If she didn't get the job…no, she didn't want to think about that until she had to. Uncaring how her behaviour could be judged, she bought a newspaper, found an air-conditioned café, ordered a Thai chicken salad, and read what movies were on while she tried to enjoy her lunch, reflecting that chicken would probably be a rare dish on a beef cattle station.

The many awards won by a recent British film persuaded her it should hold her interest, so she chose it as the best possible time-filler. Despite its glowing reputation, Angie had difficulty in following its story, which was told in innumerable flashbacks and with so many characters she couldn't get engaged with any of them. She found herself recoiling from the obsessive passion of the male lead and walked out. There was certainly no entertainment in watching a man who pursued his own desire without a care about hurting others.

The heat outside was worse. The movie had depressed her instead of distracting her and since there seemed no point in doing anything else, she caught a bus home. She felt like a limp rag by the time she let herself into the apartment. Nevertheless, it was almost five o'clock so most of the afternoon had gone.

She stripped off, took a long tepid shower, pulled on a pair of shorts and a loose singlet top, made herself a cool drink with plenty of ice and switched on the television. More entertainment, she thought ironically, as a family quiz show clicked onto the screen. She found it better than the movie, her mind harmlessly engaged in giving answers to the questions asked.

The six o'clock news was just coming on when the telephone rang. Angie leapt from her chair in a rush of nervous agitation, not having expected the call so early. Her thumb fumbled over the Off button on the remote control, finally cutting off the noise from the television so she could concentrate on whatever was said to her. She almost tripped over herself in racing to the kitchen where the telephone was installed on the wall. Pressing a hand to her thumping heart and trying to catch her breath at the same time, she lifted the receiver to her ear, hoping to hear what she desperately wanted to hear.

"Hello. Angie Cordell speaking…"

"Hi, babe!"

Instant deflation.

"I made a big killing on the floor today," Brian crowed. "Got to celebrate and who better with than you! I'm on my way right now so you've got about twenty minutes to pretty yourself up for a night on the town."

"No, Brian!" she cried in vehement protest, then in a frantic rush, "I'm busy. I can't go out. I won't. You've got to stop doing this."

The phone was dead.

Angie closed her eyes and took several deep breaths, trying to quell the onsurge of panic. She gritted her teeth in fierce determination. Brian was not going to do this to her. It had to stop.

She dialled his mobile telephone number, hoping to put him off coming. Nothing. He'd switched the power off. Which meant she would have to confront him face to face. Another argument. Angie slammed the receiver down in sheer frustration, then started to tremble.

She hated this. Hated it, hated it, hated it. Hugging herself tightly to stop the shakes, she walked through the living room, down the hallway to her bedroom, then back to the kitchen, repeating the well-worn track over and over again as she tried to settle the rage and fear in her mind.

She couldn't leave the apartment, not before the call

from Taylor Maguire. Besides, even if she did, Brian would probably sit in his car, waiting for her to come back. It only made matters worse, making her feel hunted.

If she didn't get this job, she would have to go to the police and get a restraining order against him. Though she didn't really believe that would work, either. Brian was so clever, with charm enough to fool anybody. He would make her out to be neurotic, someone who needed help. And she did!

Best not to answer the doorbell when he came, she decided. He couldn't know she hadn't gone out since his call. She didn't care if he sat in his car, waiting all night. He had no right to keep forcing himself into her life. Talking to him did no good and she especially didn't want the hassle of an argument when Taylor Maguire's call might come in the middle of it.

Though what if the telephone rang while Brian was at the door? He would hear if she answered it, yet she couldn't not answer. She'd told Taylor Maguire she would be in. Appearing unreliable would not go down well. He might change his mind. He might not give her the job anyway but she didn't want to torpedo what chance she had at getting it.

No point in stressing out about it, she told herself. She had no control over what Taylor Maguire did but Brian could be shut out. At least physically. The television was off. She had to remember not to switch any lights on. It wouldn't be dark for another hour or so. With any luck, Brian would go away, none the wiser she'd been here all the time.

Angie retreated to the kitchen and stayed there. She thought of preparing herself a meal. Her churning stomach denied any interest in it. She ate a bowl of strawberry ice-cream. Slowly. It was something to do while she waited.

At six twenty-five the doorbell rang.

Angie stood absolutely still though her heart hammered in her ears. She watched the seconds ticking around on the kitchen clock. The thin hand had only completed a half circle when the doorbell rang again, given several sharp twists this time. She looked at the telephone, willing it to stay silent. Two minutes went by.

Had he gone? Would he cruise around in his car, trying to spot her in the street, then come back to check the apartment again? She didn't dare look out a window in case he was watching. Three more minutes passed. Angie was just beginning to breathe easily when the doorbell pealed again.

Her hands clenched. Every nerve in her body screamed a protest at the continued torment. It took enormous willpower to hold control, remaining still and silent, doing absolutely nothing that might reveal her presence. The distinct, metallic sound of a key sliding into the door lock froze her mind in horror and delivered a painful kick to her heart. Disbelief warred with reality as she heard the door open.

"Angie?"

It was definitely Brian. But how had he obtained a key to her apartment?

The door closed.

He was inside.

No escape from him. No point in skulking in the kitchen. He was bound to find her sooner or later. Angie waited for outrage over his invasion of her privacy to quell the sickening fear in her stomach. It didn't work. Nothing was going to work. In blind desperation she charged into the living room to confront him. He'd actually picked up the remote control for the television, apparently prepared to make himself right at home.

"Put that down, Brian!" she commanded through clenched teeth.

He was startled to see her at first but smug satisfaction quickly superseded the surprise. "In a sulk, are we? Playing hard to get?"

She didn't need outrage. Hatred burned through her. Brian Slater might be as handsome as the devil himself with his Byronic black curls, magnetic dark eyes and a smile loaded with charisma, but Angie no longer felt the slightest attraction to him. He'd worn those feelings away with his demonic moods and self-centredness. And she was not going to play his games, not now or ever!

"Just reinforcing the *no* I gave you on the phone," she shot at him. "And don't tell me you didn't hear."

He gestured at her skimpy, casual clothes. "You're obviously doing nothing else tonight. Silly to cut off your nose to spite your face, Angie."

"It's over, Brian. Find someone else to celebrate your successes with."

He grinned at her, blithely ignoring her claim and advice. "No drugs, I promise. I've been a very good boy. The least you can do is reward me."

"How did you get the key you let yourself in with?"

He laughed. "Same old place. When you were living with me you always kept a spare key in a little magnetised tin under the fuse box. Saved you from being locked out, remember?"

Stupid to have kept the same habit. She held out her hand. "Give it to me, Brian."

"I'll put it back for you."

"Just give it to me. It's mine."

He huffed exaggerated patience and handed it over. "Now can we be reasonable?" he appealed, pouring on the charm. "I was merely coming in to wait for you. We did share an apartment for years, Angie."

"That doesn't give you any claim on this one. Or on me. Would you please leave now?"

He threw up his hands. "I just got here."

"I didn't invite you."

"Angie..." Indulgent cajoling. He lowered his hands to reach out to her as he stepped forward. "...I want to share with you. We can have a happy evening together."

"No!" She backed off, lifting her own hands to ward him away. "I've told you, Brian. I don't want to pick up our relationship again."

"You said we could be friends."

The glitter in his eyes spelled trouble but Angie refused to give in, no matter what! "That's not working out for me," she stated vehemently.

"You're truly being absurd, babe. I know there's no one else."

The telephone rang.

"Isn't there?" she threw at him to give him pause for thought, then whirled into the kitchen, hoping he would give her a breathing space in which to answer the call all her hopes were hanging on. Desperate hopes. She snatched up the receiver, darting a fearful glance at Brian who'd taken up a watchful position, leaning against the doorjamb, his eyes gloatingly confident that she couldn't get away from him.

"Hello. Angie Cordell speaking," she almost gabbled in her haste.

"Taylor Maguire, Miss Cordell." His deep voice seemed to touch a chord of sanity in a situation fraught with danger.

"Yes?" she quickly encouraged, afraid of being interrupted.

"Once again thank you for your time. I'm sorry to disappoint you, Miss Cordell, but I've decided on another applicant."

Her heart fluttered and sank. For a moment, her mind was quite blank. Then the instinct for survival tore into it. She turned her back on Brian and drove a bright lilt into her voice.

"How nice! Thank you, Taylor. Do come right on over. I'd love to see you tonight."

Silence on the other end of the line. A bubble of hysteria bounced around Angie's brain. The man would think her stark raving mad. Not that it mattered. Since he hadn't served the one critical purpose he could have served, Angie had no compunction in using him to get her out of the corner she was in. Even though it was all pretence.

She tinkled a light flirtatious laugh. "Mmmh...sounds great! It's been so hot today, I sure could do with some cooling down. I'll get my things ready to go. See you soon."

She replaced the receiver and pasted satisfaction on her face as she turned to Brian. "A man I met recently," she informed him. "A man I'm interested in, Brian. So will you please leave now?"

His face looked tight and pinched. His eyes glared fury. For a moment she thought he was teetering on the edge of physically attacking her and it was all she could do to hold a relaxed pose.

"We'll see," he said darkly, and to her intense relief, wheeled away from her and strode out of the apartment, slamming the door after him.

Angie sagged against the kitchen cupboards, blessing

the opportune call that had saved her this time. The misery of her failure to get the job would undoubtedly hit her later, but right now, she could only be grateful she was rid of a horribly threatening situation. Then suddenly remembering the security chain she ran to the door and put it on. If Brian had taken the spare key before tonight and made a copy of it, at least he couldn't get past the chain. If he tried, she would call the police.

It struck her that he wouldn't have walked in here tonight if he hadn't known her flatmates were away. There were no witnesses to what he'd done. He could swear she had invited him in. Her word against his. He was so damned clever with everything he did. And she was alone. No one to back her up for another week. If Taylor Maguire hadn't called tonight…if she hadn't thought fast enough to make him an expected witness…

Angie shuddered. Tears welled into her eyes. Her chest ached from the tension, the awful, helpless feeling of fighting a force that couldn't be reasoned with. She pushed away from the door and tottered to her bedroom, wishing it was a safe refuge, knowing it offered only temporary respite.

We'll see… She shuddered again at the dark threat in those words. Brian was sure to be out there waiting, watching to see the man who was supposed to be coming. When no one turned up…

Angie crawled onto the bed and hugged a pillow as she surrendered to a storm of weeping, unbearably pressured by what was happening to her, the rage and fear and frustration clogging her life, leaving her no room to move on to something better. The chance she'd hoped for with Taylor Maguire was gone. She had to leave here…go somewhere else…anywhere else. Job or no job, she had to get on a train or plane tomorrow and move as far away from Brian as she could. It was the only answer.

The tears kept falling, an endless well of them, grief for her own foolishness in falling for the charismatic attractions of a man who couldn't be trusted. Even before the drug-taking had distorted the darker side of his personality, there had been lies and risk-taking that went beyond easy acceptance. She had been mad to stay with him so long, to think she could change him or even influence him. Brian Slater was a law unto himself and no one was going to stop him from doing what he wanted.

The bedroom was gathering dark shadows with evening closing in. She listlessly supposed she should put on the lights, at least maintain the fiction she was expecting a visitor. Probably futile. Brian would be watching. He'd know. Though someone might arrive to call on another occupant of the apartment block. She might be lucky enough to benefit from a coincidence.

Fired by the need to capitalise on any possible mistake Brian could make, Angie scrambled off the bed and raced through the apartment, switching on lights. Breathless, her heart pumping madly, she was heading for the bathroom to wash her sticky face when the doorbell rang, almost making her jump out of her skin. She stood stock-still, trying to gather the shreds of her strength to meet this new onslaught of emotional tension.

No sound of a key sliding into the lock.

Angie forced herself to backtrack, to watch the front door, to listen for any activity on the other side of it.

The bell rang again.

She started to shake. It was a repetition of Brian's earlier call. But the chain would hold, she assured her-

CHAPTER THREE

ANGIE didn't pause to ask why a virtual stranger would care about her, care enough to investigate the strange response she'd made to his call. She thought only of Taylor Maguire's strength as she rushed to the door, strength she could lean on tonight, strength that could keep Brian away if he tried to intrude again.

She pushed the chain out of its slot and wrenched the door open wide, driven by an urgency to get the man she needed inside quickly in case Brian was following and forced a confrontation that would put her in a bad light. "It was so good of you to come," she babbled, gesturing an invitation to enter, her gaze darting past him to check if Brian was loitering on the stairs either way.

"Miss Cordell..."

He hadn't moved. He was frowning at her.

"Please..." she begged. "If you'd just come in for a while..."

He stepped past her without another word. She slammed the door shut and slotted in the security chain as fast as she could. Only then did reaction catch up with her and she leaned against the closed door, hit by the shock wave of sudden release from her torment. Safe... her mind wept with the relief of it...safe because Taylor Maguire had heard a call for help and answered it.

She gulped in a lungful of air and turned herself around to face her saviour. He was standing quite close but her eyes had difficulty in getting him into clear focus. His image wavered, swam. "Thank you," she choked out. Then her knees buckled and she was sliding down the door.

He caught her before she completely collapsed on the floor. With seemingly effortless ease he scooped her up and cradled her against his chest. Angie didn't try to struggle. She closed her eyes over the wet glaze that had distorted her vision and limply gave in to the comforting sense of being enveloped in strength.

He carried her. She couldn't even bring herself to care where. He set her down on the squashy leather sofa in the living room. Angie sank into it as his arms slid away. She wished she could sink into oblivion. It was a shaming situation. Taylor Maguire had seen her as potential trouble and he was right. She was. But she was still glad he'd come.

She heard him leave her side and panic swirled again. "Don't go!" The cry ripped from her throat as she hoisted herself up.

"Stay there! Rest!" he commanded, a figure of indomitable authority, taking charge. In a softer tone, he added, "I'll be back in a moment. You need a drink. And a facecloth."

Angie subsided, railing at her own weakness. Her judgment was hopelessly awry. This was the kind of man who took care of things, not the kind to walk away. All the same, she couldn't just lie here like dead weight and impose on his kindness. She had to think of what to do next.

Pulling herself together was the first step. There was no time to waste if she was to get away from Brian tonight. She couldn't expect Taylor Maguire to stay here with her but he could take her with him when he left, dropping her off at a hotel where she would feel safe until tomorrow. She swung her legs off the sofa and pushed herself into a sitting position, hunching over and taking deep breaths to ward off a cloud of dizziness.

The man of action returned. He didn't criticise her movement. He didn't chat. A glass of water was thrust into her hand. She drank it. He took the glass and offered her a damp washer. She wiped her face and hands, finding it refreshing.

"Thanks," she said huskily, offering him a rueful smile. "Sorry I'm such a mess. I should be offering you something."

"No need. When you feel up to it, you can tell me what's been going on here. It will help clear the air. In every sense."

Exuding efficient and stabilising purpose, he stepped over to the dining table, pulled out a chair, set it down close to her and sat, determined on putting himself in the picture.

Angie had to concede he deserved to know what he'd walked into on her behalf. Most city people wouldn't have involved themselves at all and she couldn't really blame them. It was easier not to know, not to put themselves in any firing line. This man was of a different breed. She'd known that intuitively from the first moment she saw him. Nevertheless, she was reluctant to confess the full truth. It cast her in a dubious light. She didn't know why Taylor Maguire's opinion of her counted, but it did.

"There was someone here when I rang," he prompted, apparently deciding the sooner she talked, the better.

"Yes. We were lovers once," she blurted out. Impossible to skate over that if the situation was to make sense and she needed his sympathy. "I left him because

I couldn't trust him any more. He does drugs. He denies
it now but his behaviour..." She shook her head, knowing no one could have the understanding she did. "I
won't go back to him and he won't let go."

"What happened tonight?"

"He called to say he was taking me out. I said no but
he came anyway. I had to wait in for your call but I
pretended I wasn't here. I didn't answer the doorbell. He
found where I'd left a spare key to the apartment and
let himself in."

"You didn't have the security chain on?"

She flushed at the stupid oversight. "I didn't think.
Normally I would. I was distracted...worrying about
your call...and the job." In anguished embarrassment
she rushed on. "It just didn't occur to me he'd go that
far. Maybe he knew my flatmates were away so he
wouldn't be sprung by anyone other than me. Usually
he waits outside in his car."

A beetling frown. "Is he there now?"

"Did you see a black Porsche in the street when you
arrived?"

The frown deepened. "Yes, I did."

"That's him. Waiting to see if someone turned up. It
was only the threat of you coming that got him out. He's
careful about witnesses."

"How long has this stalking been going on?"

Stalking... Angie shuddered at the horrible word. It
was all the more horrible because it described so truly
what Brian was doing to her.

"Six months," she answered bleakly.

"Have you gone to the police about it?"

She shook her head. "Brian comes from a wealthy
family. With political connections. He can slide out of
most things." Her eyes reflected the bitter irony of her

position. "I'm a nobody, Mr. Maguire. Whom do you think they'll believe? Besides, they can't enforce protection. How many times do you hear they can't do anything until a crime is committed?"

He didn't argue. "Brian who?" he asked.

"Slater."

"What's the registration number of his Porsche?"

"Triple zero MIL." She'd answered automatically, then thought it an odd question. "Why?"

"I'll get the police to move him on. At least that much can be accomplished." He stood up, so unflappably self-assured in taking direct and immediate action, it dazed Angie. "Where's your telephone?" he asked, glancing around.

"You...believe me?"

His gaze swept back to her, his piercing blue eyes unshadowed by any doubt. "I generally do believe what I see for myself, Miss Cordell. The phone?"

"On the wall in the kitchen," she answered, still stunned he was prepared to take matters into his own hands with the most minimal briefing. A man accustomed to making judgments and acting on them as fast as need be, she surmised, and wished she knew how he had made his final judgment on the governess applicants. Though it was irrelevant now. What was done was done. But she couldn't help envying the woman who had got the job.

She heard him talking in the kitchen, his voice very firm and controlled, quietly demanding, expecting respect and co-operation. He would undoubtedly get it, too. It was one of the less acceptable truths of life that men were more likely to draw an active response out of officialdom than women. And Taylor Maguire was certainly not any man.

The talking ended. He returned to the living room. "We'll be notified when he leaves," he stated with absolute confidence, no question that Brian *would* be moved on.

"Thank you for your…your intervention. May I ask another favour?"

He raised his eyebrows invitingly.

"When you leave, could I get a lift with you to a hotel? I'd prefer not to stay here tonight."

He studied her for several moments before speaking. "This was why you wanted the governess job," he said quietly.

"The main reason," she acknowledged. "Though everything else I said *was* the truth, Mr. Maguire."

He nodded. She had the impression he was satisfied he had it all slotted into place. "Are you in a fit enough state to pack what you want to take with you?"

"Yes, of course." She pushed up from the sofa and held herself steady, proving she was capable of managing. "It will only take me a few minutes to change my clothes and throw a few things into an overnight bag."

"I meant everything you don't want to leave behind. Best we take it with us so you don't have to return here. I'll book you a room at the Hilton for tonight. Tomorrow we'll fly to Giralang. It means you'll be taking up your position as governess earlier than necessary but it saves you from further harassment and me from another trip."

She gaped at him, scarcely believing her ears. "I thought you'd given the job to someone else."

An ironic smile briefly curled his lips. "The young lady I'd chosen asked me to call after eight o'clock. It's not yet eight. What you could call a fortuitous circumstance, Miss Cordell."

"But you don't want me."

The words fell from her lips and the moment they were spoken she berated herself for looking a gift horse in the mouth. He was handing her the chance she wanted, the chance she needed. Why be so self-defeating as to question it?

For some reason it raised a tension between them that hadn't been there before. On her part, it was a reluctance to accept a position he might begrudge because she wasn't his first choice, yet her whole being yearned to go with him, be with him, stay with him.

She didn't know what conflict he held within himself, but she was aware of it. His eyelids dropped, veiling any expression that might have revealed his feelings. His face was a granite mask. There was an unyielding stiffness to his stance, as though his mind would always impose its will on his body, denying it any natural impulses unless there was mental and physical harmony.

After a nerve-tearing silence, he softly said, "I would never leave any woman in your position, Miss Cordell. Whatever the cost of this decision, I'll pay it."

She flushed, pained by the idea she was costing him anything. "I'm sorry you think I'll be trouble. I'll do my best not to be, Mr. Maguire. And I truly am good with children. You won't lose by taking me, I promise."

"We'll see," he murmured. "You need not sign the contract. You might find a year too long for you."

"You doubt my staying power."

He shrugged. "Let's not labour the point. You need to get away. I'm prepared to take you. How long you stay at Giralang will be a matter of how well it works for all of us. Fair enough?"

"Yes. Thank you."

"Do you need help with suitcases? Boxes?"

"I'll manage." She gave him an ironic smile.

"You've done more than enough for me. Please feel free to use the phone and do help yourself to any food or drink in the kitchen."

His eyes suddenly warmed, giving her a funny feeling in the pit of her stomach. "You have guts, Miss Cordell. I respect that."

Nerves that had been frayed to breaking point, relaxed into a sweet melt of pleasure. "I won't let you down," she promised him and tore herself away from his strong presence to go and pack for a new and different life.

Resolution burned through her. Whatever his experience with other city people, she would prove his doubts about her wrong. Whatever it took, she would adjust to working on an outback station. Hardship, boredom, heat…she didn't care about any of the drawbacks.

She wanted to know Taylor Maguire's world.

More than that, she wanted to share it with him.

Taylor heaved a sigh of resignation and moved himself into the kitchen, vaguely thinking of the telephone calls he had to make. There was no going back on his decision now. He'd have to live with it. Somehow.

You don't want me.

The innocence in that statement was a dead-set killer to the desires she stirred. She didn't want *him* was the bald truth of it. While he had been consumed with the tantalising excitement her provocative invitation on the telephone had aroused—the chance of pursuing an attraction that still had him in its grip—she had been grasping at any straw to save herself from another man.

Of course he'd known something had to be wrong but the fact she'd reached out to him on such a personal level had muddled all sense of logic and fired what was patently an absurd fantasy—a brief but torrid affair with her, here in the city before he went home. Bitter irony. *She* certainly didn't have a sexual need crying out to be answered and she'd undoubtedly recoil violently from any suggestion of it from him.

He found himself gripping the edge of the sink. He loosened his hands and looked down at them, remembering the feel of her as he'd carried her to the sofa, the imprint of her breasts squashing against his chest, the silky smoothness of her bare thighs, the warmth of her body, its soft femininity. Despite her obvious distress, it had taken all his willpower to act as he knew he should.

Madness to take her with him to Giralang.

Continual torment.

But what else could he have done?

She'd looked so helpless, so vulnerable, so needful of protection. He could not have walked away from her very real plight, leaving her in danger of being assaulted. Or worse.

It would probably only be for a few weeks, he told himself. A month at most. A woman like Angie Cordell would want to be back in a city, once she'd had time to recover from this traumatising experience. Giralang meant no more than an escape to her. She would see it as a prison soon enough. Just as Trish had. The difference was Angie Cordell was free to move on. And she would.

Hopefully before the men returned to work.

Hopefully before he made a fool of himself, wanting what common sense told him was impossible, impractical and downright dangerous to even contemplate. Any close involvement with her at Giralang would be courting the worst kind of trouble. Fantasy and reality did not mix. He had to keep that very clear in his mind and not allow physical need to have any sway on his behaviour toward her.

His gaze fell on a bowl and spoon in the sink. They were smeared with pink ice-cream or yoghurt. He washed them up, then moved to use the wall telephone. He'd set a course of action. He had to go through with it. It was the only decent thing to do in the circumstances. He could only hope his *indecent* obsession with Angie Cordell would soon ease.

She didn't belong to his world.

She wouldn't want to, once she knew it.

CHAPTER FOUR

IT SEEMED to Angie they had been flying over a sea of red earth for a long time. Only when the altitude of the Piper Comanche dropped did she realise the landscape wasn't entirely barren. There were occasional clumps of scrubby trees, the contorted loops of a creek or river, the silver flash of water tanks that probably fed troughs for wandering stock, lines denoting roads which gave some reassurance of civilisation, albeit extremely remote.

From Brisbane they had headed northwest across Queensland to what was called the Gulf country, lying between the outback mining town of Mt. Isa—the largest silver and lead producer in the world—and the Gulf of Carpentaria. Giralang was situated on the Leichardt River, northeast of the town, and by road, about five hours' journey in a four-wheel drive distant from it. The road was currently impassable due to recent flooding.

Angie's head was swimming with the facts her new employer had related to her over earphones during the flight. Taylor Maguire was not a chatty man and she hadn't liked to engage him in too much conversation since he was piloting a plane which, to her mind, was alarmingly small. However, her curiosity about where she was going to had necessitated some questions so she could be at least mentally prepared for it.

A check of her watch assured her they must be nearing the property, if not already over it. Her mind couldn't really encompass an area of almost three thousand square kilometres, which Taylor had told her was the

size of the station on which he ran about thirty thousand
cattle, another unimaginable number. Nevertheless, she
should soon be able to spot the cluster of buildings
which he had described as like a small, self-contained
township.

Apart from the homestead, there were cottages for the
head stockman, the chief engineer, the men's cook, the
gardener, all of whom had wives, a large house for the
musterers and jackeroos, the Aborigines' settlement, a
store, a butcher's shop, schoolroom, office, equipment
sheds.

Forty-eight people were on his payroll, mostly men.
Many of them were on leave, at the moment, as it was
the wet season, during which the general work of the
station eased up. Mustering usually began again in
March. Nevertheless, Angie felt life couldn't be too
lonely at Giralang since she would be living in a community, albeit an isolated one.

Even within the homestead itself, she would not be
alone with Taylor and his son. His widowed aunt,
Thelma Winton, ran the household with the help of two
Aboriginal women, Gemma and Yvonne. Both the helicopter pilot, Gary Dawson, and the bookkeeper, Leo
Pockley, lived in. Angie had memorised these names,
hoping to save any awkwardness in greeting them over
the first few days. She was resolved on doing her utmost
to fit in and learn what was expected of her as quickly
as possible.

She glanced surreptitiously at the profile of the man
sitting beside her, taking in the high, intelligent forehead,
thickly lashed eyes narrowed to the distance ahead,
straight-line nose, a mouth that was surprisingly full-
lipped, providing a touch of softness on an otherwise
hard face, a strongly chiselled chin, slightly jutting as

though aggressively defying the arrows of fortune. It was strange how the more she saw him, the more impressively handsome he looked. She judged him to be in his mid-thirties, certainly too young to live the rest of his life without a woman.

A disquietening thought slid into her mind... How did single men in the outback manage their enforced celibacy? The occasional weekend trip to the closest town? Taylor Maguire had certainly seen her as a possible source of trouble to his men. To himself, as well? How far did sexual frustration drive a man? Perhaps, while he'd been in Brisbane... She frowned, inwardly recoiling from the idea, even though she reasoned it was a pragmatic solution to a physical need.

She caught herself glancing down at his strong, muscular thighs, wondering what he'd be like as a lover, and felt an uncomfortable stab of guilt over the speculation. Guilt and shock. She couldn't afford to even begin to think along such lines. It was courting trouble which neither of them wanted.

Besides, he had probably been deeply attached to his wife. With their son, Hamish, being seven now, the relationship had been a long-standing one, harder to let go than hers and Brian's, especially when death didn't offer a choice. There was no such thing as a *clean break*, she realised. Emotions lingered on.

"There it is, straight ahead."

His deep voice boomed through her earphones, jolting Angie out of her reverie. Her gaze fastened on what looked like an oasis in the middle of a desert, a startling patch of green with large, full-grown trees providing shade for a group of buildings, the biggest of which had Giralang printed across its roof.

"How do you maintain a lawn?" she asked in wonder.

"Sprinkler system from the dam."

"What about drought?" He'd told her the wet season was followed by nine months of dry weather, which seemed a long time without rain.

"We have enough bores to see us through a serious drought," came the matter-of-fact reply.

Artesian bores, tapping into the great underground basin of water which lay beneath the outback, the remnant of an inland sea of ancient times. What would happen if it ever ran out, Angie thought fancifully, or were there endless supplies trapped by the earth?

As they came in to land, she noticed the buildings were set out in a grid pattern—very orderly—and were all painted white with green roofs and trim, and green water tanks attached to them, giving a uniform look that was neat and attractive and denoted a caring pride in the place. The Maguire family had owned Giralang since the last century. It was a hands-on operation and always had been, unlike the many cattle stations owned by pastoral companies and run by managers who came and went. It must make a difference, Angie reasoned. There was always more pride in actual ownership.

She held her breath as the plane touched down on the red clay airstrip but the landing went smoothly and she relaxed as it slowed to a halt, adjacent to a huge shed. Her relief at having arrived safely, however, was mingled with a sense of trepidation over the next step in her introduction to Taylor Maguire's world. A Jeep was being driven out to meet them.

"Hamish and Leo," Taylor said, waving to the occupants.

His son and the bookkeeper. Akubra hats, drawn

down low on their foreheads, shaded their features, making it impossible for Angie to see what they looked like, apart from the obvious of being a man and a boy.

Trying to quell the nervous excitement playing havoc with her insides, Angie followed Taylor out of the cockpit and waited for him to open the door. Her new life would revolve around the boy she was about to meet. It would help enormously if she could make a favourable impression.

She snatched her straw hat up from the seat she'd dropped it on, glad she had thought to leave it out of her packing. Clearly hats were the order of the day. Taylor had not commented on her appearance so she hoped what she had considered a sensible, unobtrusive choice of clothes for the trip would meet general approval.

The almost knee-length fawn shorts had seemed both modest and practical for climbing in and out of a small plane. She wore a fawn and white striped shirt over a white singlet, tying the ends casually at her waist. The white walkers on her feet were definitely activity shoes, nothing fancy about them. She might not look exactly "country" but it was the best she could do with what she had.

The door swung open. Taylor made his exit first, ready to render her assistance if she needed it since it was quite a stretch to the ground and only one step to lessen the distance.

"Have you got the new computer, Dad?"

The eager burst of natural excitement from the boy was an encouraging sign of welcome.

"Yes, it's on board, Hamish," Taylor assured him matter-of-factly. "I'll need a hand with it, Leo."

"Figured you would," came the laconic reply.

There was no move away to hug the child, no gesture of warmth or affection extended to either party. Taylor turned straight to Angie, beckoning her down, and dryly stated, "I've brought the new governess, as well."

No burst of excitement greeted this piece of news. No comment, either. Angie backed out of the plane to a silence that twanged on her every nerve. She pasted a determined smile on her face, planted her feet firmly on the ground, then swung around to meet the appraisals being made of her.

Shock on both faces, old and young.

"Angie, this is Leo Pockley. Leo, Angie Cordell."

The formal introduction jolted the bookkeeper into an acknowledgment, though he threw a look of disbelief at Taylor as he stepped forward to offer his hand. "Pleased to meet you, Miss," he mumbled, using the tipping of his hat in courtesy to evade meeting her eyes. Whether he was hopelessly shy or deeply disconcerted by her appearance, it was impossible to tell.

"Thank you, Leo. And please call me Angie," she said, trying to project warmth as she pressed his hand.

Taylor had told her informality was the general rule of the station, everyone using first names, including the children. She shouldn't feel uncomfortable with it, but Leo Pockley's obvious discomfort with her made her feel as though she was being too forward. He was a short, stocky man, grey-haired, with a deeply grooved face which placed him in his fifties. He ducked his head and stepped back smartly, as though her touch had burnt him.

"And this is Hamish," Taylor went on, apparently unperturbed by the impact she was making.

Angie turned to the boy, her smile still firmly in place. No smile from him. No move toward her. He was tall for his age, and very like his father, though his features were yet to harden and fine, and he was unskilled in guarding his expression. His face had mutiny stamped all over it; jutting chin, compressed lips, hostile distrust glaring from his eyes.

"Say hello to Angie, Hamish." It was a command, softly spoken but a firm command, nonetheless.

It evoked a flash of defiance, the boy's gaze briefly locking with his father's, challenging his dominating authority before visibly resigning himself to it. Angie took the initiative, saving his pride a little in making the greeting easier by stepping forward and holding out her hand to him. "Hello, Hamish."

"Hello," he repeated grudgingly, his eyes hating the trap of a courteous handclasp but unable to completely flout good manners under his father's eye. He left Angie with little doubt of rebellion at a later date, when she was the only supervisor.

Angie didn't try to make conversation with the boy while the men transferred her luggage and the box containing the new computer from the plane to the Jeep. She saw no point in inviting a contentious display of rudeness. Experience had taught her if she stood back and declined to force anything, children's curiosity and desire for attention usually drove them to cross the barriers they themselves had erected. Being ignored got under their skin more effectively than all the coaxing in the world.

Nevertheless, it was hardly a propitious start, Angie thought, hoping Taylor was prepared to be patient, too, and not judge the trouble factor too quickly. He knew she had nowhere else to go. Before they'd left Brisbane this morning, she'd posted a letter of resignation to the headmaster of the school where she had been employed.

Another letter, containing a cheque for a month's rent, had informed her flatmates she had left and they could relet her room to someone else. Her bridges were comprehensively burnt.

Despite the thickness of her hair, her scalp felt as though it was getting burnt, too. The midafternoon heat out here on the airstrip was intense. Definitely hat country, Angie decided, cramming hers on her head. She rolled down her shirt sleeves and buttoned them at her wrist, suddenly seeing the sense of the cover-up, protective clothing worn by the others. It was a relief to get in the Jeep and be moving again.

On the positive side of the ledger, Angie was quite enchanted by the drive up to the homestead. There were not only lawns and trees around the buildings, but a stunning array of bougainvillea, massive cascades of colour; pinks, oranges, scarlets, purples and white. She spotted several banana groves and exotic African tulip trees.

Even more amazing was a satellite dish. They were obviously not technologically backward here. After Taylor's crack about entertainment on tap, she hadn't dared ask about television, but it would seem they did have it. There was no lack of comfort, either. Air-conditioning units were set into the windows of living areas. They might be occupying a primitive world in some senses but this was certainly an oasis of modern civilisation.

When they pulled up in front of the homestead, Angie was more amazed. The house could have graced a luxurious block on beach frontage at the Gold Coast. Double-storeyed, it had a deep veranda on both levels, with bougainvillea draped beautifully over the top railings. Double sliding-glass doors dressed the long frontage, denoting its relatively recent construction, and all doors and windows were gauzed against insects.

Angie reasoned this house must have replaced a much older homestead, which might have been more interesting in a historical sense, but she was not about to complain about being misled about life in the outback. She was only too pleased to have modern amenities.

A wide expanse of lawn and garden was fenced and the Jeep pulled up beside the gate which opened to the path leading to the front entrance of the house. They piled out. Leo Pockley offered to carry in Angie's luggage. Hamish hung back with him. Taylor opened the gate and waved Angie forward. Unbelievably there were old established rosebushes growing along strips of garden on either side of the path.

Angie was in a state of awe as she was ushered into a wide hallway. The cooler air inside the house reminded her to remove her hat. The floor was tiled and there were exotic indoor plants in lovely urns on either side of the front door.

"I'll take you to meet my aunt. She'll show you to your room and see you settled," Taylor informed her as he led her past a staircase and to a huge, splendidly equipped kitchen at the rear of the house.

The warm, friendly smell of freshly baked cookies wafted to her, drawing a natural smile. Two Aboriginal women, one rolling pastry on a marble slab, one at the sink washing dishes, paused in their work, responding with wide grins, their dark eyes sparkling with interest. The third woman in the kitchen froze in the act of opening a can of fruit, her whole body stiffening in shock.

She was tall and spare, iron-grey hair pulled back into a knot, her strong-boned face holding the sag of age well though she looked to be in her sixties. Her slacks and long-sleeved shirt gave her a mannish air of authority, more so perhaps because the other women were plump and wearing loose shift dresses. Angie's mind was bombarded with a host of quick impressions, but the overriding one was the almost blank recoil in the grey eyes staring at her.

"Thelma, this is Angie Cordell, our new governess," Taylor dropped into the charged silence.

The grey eyes snapped from Angie to him and their expression clearly questioned his sanity.

Taylor ignored it. "Yvonne... Gemma..." he introduced.

They bobbed their heads, apparently too shy to say anything.

"Yvonne's daughter, Jessie, and Gemma's son, Wayne, will be taking lessons with you," he went on.

"I'm pleased to meet you," Angie said as pleasantly as she could, conscious of waves of disapproval coming from Thelma Winton. "And I look forward to meeting Jessie and Wayne," she pushed out, struggling to remain calm and composed.

"You'll find my Jessie a good girl. Quiet," Yvonne informed proudly.

Gemma laughed. "Not Wayne. That boy can't keep still."

"Boys always tend to be more lively than girls," Angie said warmly, relieved to have some of the ice broken. The lack of any friendly comment from Taylor's aunt, however, was disheartening.

"Leo's taking Angie's luggage upstairs, Thelma," Taylor prompted.

"Yes. Well..." The words were clipped out. The can opener was discarded. A glare at Taylor said *on your head, be it,* then a stiff smile that didn't reach her eyes was directed at Angie. "You must be tired after your long trip. And in need of refreshing yourself."

"Yes, I am," she agreed ruefully, aware that disagreement would be unacceptable. Thelma Winton couldn't get rid of her fast enough, no doubt wanting to give Taylor an earful on his choice of governess.

"Gemma, prepare a tray. A plate of those cookies and a pot of tea. Or do you prefer coffee, Angie?" she rattled out briskly.

"No. Tea will be fine, thank you."

"Milk and sugar?"

"Yes, please."

"Bring the tray upstairs to the room you prepared this morning, Gemma. Yvonne, you supply Taylor with whatever he wants." She swept past the other two women. "Come, my dear, I'll show you where everything is so you can settle in."

Angie looked at Taylor who'd stepped aside to clear a path for his aunt. She caught his gaze and despite the plummeting of her spirits at the less than friendly reception from those she would be living with, she could still sincerely say, "Thank you for everything, Taylor."

He returned a wry little smile, his eyes acknowledging it wasn't easy for her. "I hope it's worth it to you."

She barely had time to nod, having to fall in with his aunt's brisk injunction to, "Come along now." Nevertheless, just that brief exchange made her feel better... the flow of understanding between them.

Taylor Maguire knew where she was coming from. He'd given her the chance she'd wanted, against his better judgment on her suitability for the position—a judgment that was obviously being echoed by those closest to him—and now it was a case of sink or swim on her own. He would be fair but he wouldn't prop her up.

There was no place for molly-coddling in the outback, Angie reasoned, respecting his stance and determined on winning his respect.

Everyone's respect, she added grittily.

Her room was charming, the furnishings mostly green and white with a splash of lemon, creating a light, bright and cheerful environment. She was provided with a double bed, writing desk, bookshelves, a couple of armchairs and a small coffee table, and appropriate lamps for reading or writing. Her luggage was stacked at the end of the bed and a wall-length built-in cupboard offered plenty of storage space. Her own small bathroom was a bonus she wasn't expecting.

"Are there any water restrictions?" she asked, wary of inadvertently earning criticism.

"Not at the moment. We've had good rain so far in this wet season. When the dry comes...well, we'll see." Thelma Winton's dismissive shrug more or less said it was pointless looking that far ahead. The scepticism in her eyes suggested Angie wouldn't last long enough to be worried by water shortage. "Is there anything else you need?"

"No. Thank you. I'm sure I'll be very comfortable here."

A sardonic twitch of the mouth. "Dinner is at seven. I expect you'll want to rest until then. If you need to find me, I'll be in the kitchen."

"Thank you again."

A curt nod. She was already at the door when the sheer weight of the unspoken rejections got the better of Angie's sense of discretion. She had always heard the hospitality of outback people was legendary. The need to know why she was being shut out of it was compelling.

"Mrs. Winton… Thelma…" She found the first name rule difficult to apply in the face of patent disapproval.

The older woman half-turned, one eyebrow raised in impatient inquiry.

Angie took a deep breath and quietly asked, "What's wrong with me?"

It caught her full attention. For a moment Angie thought she saw a flicker of respect before a look of soul-weariness dulled the grey eyes. "This is no place for a city sophisticate," she said flatly. Her gaze mockingly swept Angie from head to foot. "You're stamped with city style. Whatever lure this job had for you…the glamour of a cattle king and his kingdom…it's simply not tenable. I can only hope you won't do too much damage before you decide you've had enough."

"Damage…?" Angie frowned over the word. "I assure you…"

"If Taylor wants to be a fool, I can't stop him," she broke in bitterly. "Just don't take your frustrations with your life here out on the children. Hamish had more than enough of that from his mother."

The shock was Angie's this time. Had Taylor's wife been a city person who'd come to hate being away from it?

Thelma Winton's eyes hardened to grey slate. "I'll see you gone before I'll let that happen again, believe me. The boy deserves better."

Having delivered her baleful warning, Taylor's aunt stepped outside the room and closed the door firmly behind her.

Angie stared at it, realising she'd inherited a legacy of distrust from a dead woman.

Trouble was Taylor's word for it.

A fearful reserve from Leo Pockley.

Hostility from Hamish.

Downright condemnation from Thelma Winton.

The ironic thought came to her... *Welcome to Giralang!*

Nevertheless, there was one big consolation she could hug to herself for both immediate and lasting comfort. Brian Slater wasn't here.

CHAPTER FIVE

THE rain would pelt down any moment now, Taylor thought, glancing at the heaviness of the clouds overhead. He was glad they'd got the helicopter grounded before the downpour started, pleased also they were having a good wet this year. As he and Gary strode up the road from the airstrip, he saw the children racing from the schoolroom to the house, obviously aware of the imminent drenching.

He checked his watch. Just three-thirty. Lessons over for the day. Angie hadn't emerged with the children, he noted, despite the threatening storm. She'd taken to staying in the schoolroom, long after she needed to be there. No joy with Thelma, he supposed. Not that he could blame his aunt for her attitude. There was good reason for it, as well he knew.

"You know, Angie might like a ride in the helicopter," Gary remarked, a lilt of hopeful interest in his voice. "Give her a good view of the place."

Warning bells went off in Taylor's mind. Gary was twenty-seven, a highly skilled helicopter pilot at mustering cattle, earning good money. Of course he'd think he might have a reasonable chance with a woman who'd accepted a governess position.

He was a pleasant, cheerful, happy-go-lucky kind of guy who went out of his way not to hurt anyone. As for looks, nothing objectionable there...sandy hair, lively eyes, open friendly face, an infectious grin, well-muscled body...

57

"She saw it all when I flew her in," Taylor said bruskly, recoiling from the image of any other body but his tangling with Angie Cordell's.

"Yeah. Right. Didn't think of that."

He was thinking of other things, though, getting ready to test his luck.

"Hope you don't mind me asking, Taylor—" Gary gave him a sideways look, loaded with meaning "—but is there something on between you two? I don't want to put my foot in it."

Taylor silently cursed. He should have been ready for it. The question was inevitable, especially with the younger men due back next week. Gary had come in ahead of them, specifically to do a check on the boundary fences and bores, targeting trouble spots for attention. It was only natural he'd want to get in first claim with Angie. If it was viable.

Was it? Taylor wondered. Was she over the bastard who'd been stalking her? She'd been here a month and all that time he'd been aware of a tense reserve in her whenever she was in his company, not inviting nor encouraging an involvement with him.

But the connection *was* there. It didn't matter how much he tried to suppress the attraction he felt, his hormones buzzed in her presence. He suspected hers did, too. Her gaze was averted too carefully from him. The distance she kept so rigidly was charged with awareness.

"Leave her be, Gary," he said decisively.

A huff expressed both disappointment and resignation. "Right you are," came the grudging agreement. "Just wanted to know."

Taylor felt his chest tighten. He shouldn't be giving a *hands off* order. He knew damned well it wasn't for her protection. He'd felt the hit in the groin the moment he laid eyes on her in the Atrium Room of the Brisbane Hilton. Worse in her apartment that night when she'd guilelessly said...*you don't want me.*

He did.

No point in denying it to himself.

Though what the hell he was going to do about it... He'd be a fool to do anything at all after his experience with Trish! Thelma was right about that. It wouldn't work. Not in the long run. But did it have to be the long run?

Angie might be willing to accept a short-term affair. Take it for what it was worth while it was good for them. Was she the kind of woman who took such experiences in her stride? City society seemed to lean that way and she had certainly had one lover. At least when whatever they shared had run its course, she could be assured he wouldn't stalk her like that city scum.

Though this could all be wishful thinking on his part. He didn't know what was going on inside her head. While she gave every appearance of wanting to settle in here and do a good job—she was being extremely conscientious about the latter—might it not all stem from a sense of obligation to him for helping her out of a wretched situation?

She could hate the place—want no ties to it—and pride and gratitude were forcing her to carry on as best she could. The sense of connection to him might be an unwelcome attraction she chose to fight, a complication she didn't need or want. He really should offer to release her from the job instead of thinking how to get release for the desire she stirred.

"She sure is a looker," Gary muttered, lustful admiration in his voice.

Taylor grimaced. Gary was only stating the obvious,

so reprimanding him was ridiculous. Any woman with
Angie's attributes was trouble. Every man on the station
would probably have fantasies about her. No avoiding
that. The only way to defuse worse problems was to put
her out of reach.

"Angie's been through a bad experience, Gary," he
said, giving him a look of serious intent. "Any ribald
comments from the men and you spread the word she is
to be treated with the utmost respect. One whiff of sexual harassment and the culprit will be off this station so
fast you won't see his dust."

Gary's eyes widened, struck by the force of this ad-
monition. "I'll let 'em know, boss," he said quickly and
kept any further thoughts to himself.

Taylor felt a stab of guilt. He didn't have the right to
make judgments for Angie. It was quite possible she
could find Gary attractive. The interest of a younger man
might suit her a lot better than...

No, dammit! It would drive him up the wall watching
her with someone else. The chemistry was there for
them. He knew it. And if he was going to act on it, it
was best done now before the men arrived and started
competing for her attention.

A heavy raindrop plopped on the road in front of him,
raising steam from the heat of the gravel. Others started
hitting the ground with force. "Better sprint for it,
Gary," he urged. "I'm going to stop off at the school-
house."

"See you later then," he answered, getting a spurt on
to beat the rain.

Taylor paused a moment. He was hot and sweaty from
the day's long business. So what! he tersely dismissed,
edgy with a sudden rise in tension. He only meant to

talk to her…get a grasp on how she was feeling about the place…the difficulties she'd faced so far…if she wanted to stay on.

It was time for them to talk.

CHAPTER SIX

THE rain started thundering on the corrugated iron roof. Angie shook her head at the noise. She'd never known rain like it, such consistently hard, drenching downpours, literally battering in their ferocity. The other odd thing was how storms came and went without changing the temperature. Heat was a constant here. It would have been hell to work in this schoolroom without the air conditioner.

A thump on the porch startled her into looking up from her notes, just as the door burst open and Taylor Maguire poured into the room, permeating it with his strong presence, squeezing her heart as though he left it no space to continue its normal, orderly beating. He took off his hat, shook it free of raindrops, hung it on a peg and turned to her, a rueful smile adding its attraction to his air of intense vitality.

"Almost made it," his deep voice hummed at her, making every nerve in her body vibrate with pleasure.

"Closest port in the storm?" she queried, doubting he would actually choose to be alone with her. Why invite trouble? Trouble for both of them!

The comfort zone he had initially evoked with her was long gone, whittled away by an ever-increasing awareness of his almost overpowering masculinity. Whether he sensed the stirring of primitive female instincts in her or not, Angie was extremely conscious of her own supercharged state whenever she was with him. He wasn't entirely relaxed with her, either.

His gaze locked directly onto hers, piercing blue eyes denying her any evasion. "I wanted the opportunity to speak to you out of the earshot of others. This seemed as good a place and time as any."

Apprehension sent pinpricks down her spine. Her mind whirled in panicky embarrassment. Was he aware of how strongly attracted she was to him? Had he sought this private talk to bring it up and dispose of any hopes she might be nursing? A desperate need to keep her feelings for him hidden forced her to maintain the calmest demeanor she could manage.

"Is there some problem?" she asked, pretending total ignorance of any.

He shrugged. "Many, I would think. Though you've kept them to yourself, so I don't really know."

He didn't *know*. The panic receded. Nevertheless, his air of purpose stirred a deep unease which steadily increased as he strolled forward, passing by the children's tables, coming to face her across her desk, propping himself casually on the front edge of it. Angie immediately leaned back in her chair, feeling at a disadvantage, agitated by his closeness. Was it meant to test her reaction to him?

"The question is..." he went on, his eyes relentlessly probing. "...Do you feel you can cope with them or are they wearing you down?"

Angie took a deep breath, struggling to keep calm. There was no signed contract protecting her position. Had he mentally given her a month's trial and this was assessment day? Was he looking for an excuse to remove her from the station before the mustering team arrived next week?

He couldn't point to any trouble she'd made so far because none had arisen. On the other hand, there was only one young man on the station at the moment, Gary Dawson, the helicopter pilot. And *he* had been eyeing her up. Angie had been blandly polite to him, absolutely nothing more. But Gary might have made some comment to Taylor which he'd interpreted as trouble starting.

Resentment stirred, fed by the sense of injustice that had been eating at her ever since Thelma Winton had revealed the prejudice she held, undoubtedly shared by Taylor to some extent. Enough to prevent him from treating her to anything more than the kindly consideration one would offer a guest.

"What problems do you imagine I have?" she asked, deliberately tossing the question back at him. If he wanted to draw some damning information out of her own mouth, he could think again.

A few nerve-tearing moments passed as he weighed the challenge, appraising the golden glitter of the shield she'd pushed over her amber eyes, silently testing it with the strength of his will. She refused to give in.

"How are you finding the schoolwork?" he eventually asked.

"A new and interesting experience. The school of the air sessions are quite marvellous, giving the children the sense of belonging to a larger group and communicating with them. The correspondence sets they do are a good test of what they're learning. It's very satisfying for me to have the time to give plenty of individual attention to each pupil, since I have only three."

Let him find fault with that!

"No problems with the children?"

He meant Hamish, but Angie took her time getting to his troublesome son. "Jessie is a model pupil, diligent in her work, always wanting to please. Wayne is hyperactive, tends to be disruptive, revels in distraction. He needs a bit of carrot on the stick to do his work. I've instigated a system of rewards with him. The computer is the best carrot. He loves playing on it.''

Angie paused, wondering if Hamish had confided anything of what had gone on in the schoolroom to his father. The boy was fiercely self-contained—unnaturally so, in Angie's opinion—she doubted he opened up to anyone. From what she had observed at mealtimes, his relationship with his father was strained, based more on an obedient respect for authority than love.

''Hamish?'' Taylor prompted.

It was tricky ground for her. Perhaps a blast of honesty was needed, Angie thought, on the child's behalf, even if it did acknowledge problems Taylor might stack against her.

''Initially he was hostile, belligerent and destructive,'' she stated bluntly.

''Destructive?'' It brought a deep frown.

''On one of the first correspondence sets he scrawled swear words over every sheet. Drew dirty pictures.''

''Why wasn't I told?'' The demand was curt and angry.

''Because he was testing me, not you, Taylor. But what you might find of interest is... Hamish expected to be hit for it. He was already ducking as I picked up the papers.''

His face tightened. There was to be no opening up from him on sensitive areas of his life. She knew before he opened his mouth he would make no reply to the implied accusation of previous abuse.

''How did you handle it?'' he asked tersely.

''Well, if Hamish wanted to shock or upset me, it didn't work. I went straight for an appeal to his pride. Did he really want to send it in to the correspondence centre with his name on it? Was it how he wanted to present it amongst all the other children's work?"

"What was his response?"

"Defiant at first. By the end of the day, he'd had second thoughts. Since he'd defaced the whole set, I brought up the word processing program on the computer and helped him type out a fresh copy. He did the work and that was that."

Respect in his eyes. "He hasn't tried it again?"

"No. We have other little battles. He's very intelligent, constantly challenging."

"Still hostile?"

"Less so. I don't rise to the bait."

"You don't find it wearing?"

Angie felt her hackles rising. He was still looking for something to hang on her. "A teacher's job is always wearing," she said pertinently. "Children can have very complex personalities. I believe it's worth my time, trying to get the best out of them."

No joy for him in that little speech, Angie thought savagely.

"I notice you stay here long after lessons have ended."

"Why not? It's my domain. I feel comfortable here."

"Are you uncomfortable elsewhere?"

Angie silently cursed herself for giving him something to seize on. Though he had to know, had to realise she couldn't feel comfortable in Thelma Winton's kitchen with the chill of disapproval ever constant in the watching grey eyes. The woman didn't bother hiding it.

"I like to wind down from the day," she answered. "I also keep a journal. Writing my thoughts helps to clarify them."

"A rather lonely occupation," he remarked.

"I don't find it so. I enjoy words."

Impasse. He nodded thoughtfully, veiling his eyes. Angie remained tense, waiting for his next line of attack. The top half of his shirt was wet and her gaze was inexorably drawn to where the damp fabric clung to him, delineating the disturbing maleness of his physique, the strongly muscled shoulders, broad chest. Whorls of black hair were flattened against his skin in the opened V of his shirt, just below the base of his neck. She wondered if his chest was matted with them, how it would feel to...

"Do you *want* to ride?"

The soft question startled and confused her, striking as it did through thoughts of sexuality, seeming to hit on the desires she struggled to suppress. Angie felt herself blushing and could barely meet his eyes as the rack of her uncertainties screwed itself up another notch.

"I beg your pardon?" she gabbled out, realising almost instantly he couldn't have been dabbling in sexual innuendo.

"Joe says you're frightened of horses but you're gamely persisting with the riding lessons," Taylor elaborated.

Joe Cameron, the head stockman, whose services as a riding instructor had been offered by his wife, Sue, the first week Angie was here. The school term hadn't been due to begin until February, the children frequently took off on their horses, and Sue had advised if Angie wanted mobility around the station, she'd best learn to ride.

"I'm not exactly frightened. More intimidated," she said defensively. "I've never had anything to do with horses before coming here. Up close they're big, and once I'm in the saddle, it feels a long way from the ground, but I *am* getting used to it."

"You don't have to, Angie," he said quietly.

"I want to," she insisted.

She wanted to ride to the river with the children and not be a total greenhorn in the saddle. It was even more important to her to scratch off the label of "a city person" who had no "country" skills at all.

He measured the set look on her face and murmured, "Pride goes before a fall."

"And determination picks you up again," she retorted.

It evoked a quirky smile. "So it does. I was just wondering if your determination was misplaced. Forcing yourself to do something that goes against your grain is really a waste of energy that could be channelled into a more productive area for you."

"Well, I guess I should be the judge of that," she said, resentment simmering again at his obvious lack of faith in her adjusting to the parameters of this environment. "Did Joe say I was wasting his time?" she asked, wanting to pin down this inquisition.

"No." Another quirky smile. "He admires your guts."

That was a relief. She liked Joe. He was a short, wiry man who'd lived all his forty-something years in the bush, his weathered face and bandy legs testifying that most of them had been spent on a horse. He was patient, good-humoured, always ready to smooth over her mistakes or nervousness with a joke.

"Then have I done something wrong?" she persisted, wishing Taylor would emit a sense of camaraderie instead of holding an impenetrable reserve.

"Not at all," he assured her. "I would say a lot of things right. You seem to be fitting into our little community very well. I've heard only good things about you.''

''They're nice people,'' she said sincerely. Only the Maguire family kept her shut out of their hearts. Everyone else had been kind and helpful, offering open hospitality and happy to give her the benefit of their experience.

''Yes,'' he agreed. ''Though I appreciate it's taken considerable effort from you. It is a world away from what you're used to.''

The control Angie had been exerting over her feelings snapped. He wasn't as blatant as his aunt in his prejudice against her but she'd felt it coming through every word he'd spoken and she didn't deserve any of it. Her frustrations boiled over and the words flew out with almost violent vehemence.

''Don't judge me by your wife!''

It hit him full-on, like a slap in the face. His jaw jerked. A flicker of some dark emotion destroyed the steady power of his probing gaze. Compelled now to drive her point home and goaded beyond endurance by judgments that were not relevant to her, Angie slammed her hands on the desk and stood up, leaning forward in a burst of turbulent aggression.

''No two people are the same. Everyone's life is shaped differently. If you don't know that, you're a man of very limited vision. So I come from the city as your wife did! That doesn't stop me from being an individual in my own right, and I'm fed up with being dumped on because of a hangover from your marriage.''

She straightened up, proudly defiant, furiously angry with the situation. ''I'm *me*. Angie Cordell. And it's time you took the blinkers off your eyes, Taylor Maguire.''

Then she whirled away from him, too agitated by the explosive expulsion of her emotions to keep facing him.

The storm outside hadn't yet eased. There was nowhere to go. She stopped at the window, staring blindly at the torrential rain beating the ground, her arms hugging her midriff to hold in the churning mire of her insides. The thundering on the roof was almost deafening but it wasn't as loud as the silence behind her. Her skin crawled with her awareness of it, the risk she'd taken, the outcome pending.

She told herself she didn't care. He hadn't been openly honest with her about the situation she was walking into. While she was still grateful to him for getting her away from Brian, that was in the past now, and this was what she was living with, and she didn't regret blowing the lid off the truth. Taylor wasn't being fair to her. Neither was his aunt, nor his son. Though she didn't blame the boy for the sins of his parents.

She hated the thought of his wife.

It hurt. It hurt to be put in the same box as her. Dismissed and rejected and loaded with her crimes, whatever they were. It just wasn't fair! She'd lived too long with unfairness from Brian and she simply wasn't up to copping any more of it.

"Apart from telling you when and how she died, I haven't mentioned my wife." The quiet words held a note of perplexity.

"Thelma did," she answered flatly.

"I see."

"I guess you could say she spelled out what you didn't."

"I'm sorry. I didn't realise…"

"At least it made sense of the interview for me."

No comment.

"You want me to go, don't you? You've given me a month's respite and now you want me to leave and channel my energies somewhere else."

"I didn't say that, Angie."

"You were working your way around it." Bitterness at his tactics spewed the suspicion. "Do you have your first choice of governess waiting in the wings?"

"No. I said I'd give you a chance."

"Have you?" She swung around to face him with it. "Have you really, Taylor?"

He hadn't moved. He didn't move now except to make a gesture of appeasement. "Angie, I was merely trying to ascertain how you felt, after being here for a month."

"Then let me tell you your cynicism was shining through every word."

He frowned, shook his head. "I didn't mean to hurt you." The blue eyes fastened on hers with devastating sincerity. "I truly did not come in here to take you down or suggest you leave."

Her heart jiggled painfully. He might be speaking the truth but the judgments were still there, the judgments that ruled his attitude toward her, that kept her shut out of his life, denied any real sharing with him, denied his confidence and trust. She didn't know why it meant so much to her but it did. It did. And the need to fight for justice from him was as much a raging torrent inside her as the rain outside.

"Have I let you down in any shape or form?" she fired at him.

"No. You've exceeded my expectations," he conceded softly.

"Have I caused any trouble?"

An ironic twist. "You've been a model of decorum, Angie."

"Leo Pockley came from the city." He'd told her he'd been a computer programmer who'd worked for the one company for twenty-five years, only to be retrenched at fifty, too old to be easily employable again in that field. Widowed, his children settled in their own careers, he'd made a new life for himself as the bookkeeper on Giralang. "He loves it here," she stated pointedly.

"He feels useful again, Angie."

"But he's fitted in."

"Yes."

"I'm told some of your jackeroos come from the city, too. They soon adjust to the life."

"It's what they want to do. You were escaping, Angie...not coming to...running away from. There's a difference."

"So what?" she fiercely retaliated, her arms flying out to punctuate her argument. "You know perfectly well a city person can adjust to the outback, can fit in and like it. We're not all the same. It's because I'm a woman that you're all cockeyed about it." Then with reckless disregard to what she stirred in him, she demanded, "Do I look like your wife?"

"No!" His face twisted with hatred and he came off the desk in an explosive rejection of the suggestion, his hand slicing the air in agitated dismissal. "You don't know what you're talking about."

"Well, I'll tell you this, Taylor Maguire," she shot back at him. "You don't know me. You haven't even tried to know me. And until you do, your judgments of me aren't worth anything!"

"Aren't they?" he snapped. "What are yours worth, Angie?"

His eyes blazed at her as he moved with fast, efficient intent, skirting the tables to make straight for where she stood by the window. Angie had a vivid impression of power, danger, emotions unleashed and fiercely encompassing her. It pumped her heart faster. She stared at him, unable to look away, unable to speak, her throat constricting, her mind buzzing with the mad excitement of having broken his control, and a wild shoot of joy and longing went through her, making her tingle with anticipation.

She felt a great shifting violent force, gathering momentum as he moved nearer, and she had a sense of chaos let loose and didn't care. She revelled in it. The noise of the rain receded, as though they were being sucked into a whirling vacuum where only she and he existed. Then he was right in front of her, dominating everything, scooping her against him, and she was not just looking at him but absorbing him with all her senses.

She felt the strength in the arms locking her to him, the rock-hardness of his body, smelled—almost tasted—the outback land that owned him, the heat, the sweat, the steamy rain, the aggressive maleness that took it all in its stride. The only sound she heard was his breathing, heavy and strangely intimate this close to her, his chest rising and falling against her breasts. Otherwise stillness, except for his eyes exploring hers with the intensity of raw need reaching out, wanting it reflected.

She didn't know what he saw. The frustration, the hurt, the jealousy, the fear, the thwarted desires… Every turbulent emotion that had contributed to this moment were all centred deep inside her, yet swamping them was a physical thing, a huge vibrant overwhelming rush of sexuality, more powerful than she had ever experienced.

In slow motion it seemed, he bent his head and began

to kiss her, carefully at first, then slightly harder, his tongue feathering her lips, pushing past them. She quivered with pleasure, her response instant, instinctively encouraging. He seized on it, his mouth possessing hers in a storm of erotic passion, and Angie closed her eyes and gave herself up to a swarm of sensation.

She felt it in every part of her, a kiss like no other she had ever known, as though it formed a stream that flowed into every corner of her body, every hidden place. She felt it bursting through her head, pouring down her throat, tingling in her breasts, swirling around her heart, throbbing through her pelvis, racing down her legs.

Her arms were around his neck, hands clutching his head to hers. She felt him cup her buttocks, urging her, moulding her closer to him, exulted in the desire coursing through him, the sheer physical strength of it, and the heat, the aching hunger it aroused in her. His hands dropped to her thighs, dragging on them, gathering up the fabric of her skirt. Then suddenly they stilled. He broke the kiss. He gripped her hips and set her back from him.

Angie moaned at the abruptness of his withdrawal, opened her eyes in anguished protest, and found him staring at her, looking shocked, almost disbelieving. She stared back at him, too dazed to wonder what he was thinking. Her whole body felt strange, shaken. Her legs ached. Her head was light, dizzy.

He dragged in a deep breath. It shuddered out. Angie wasn't sure she was breathing at all. Her eyes clung to his, needing him to make sense of what had happened. She saw his shock overtaken by conscious decision, and the fierce desire to carry the decision through.

"I want to know you, Angie," he said gruffly, his

deep voice echoing through her mind, drawing its ragged edges into some coherency. "I take it you want to know me."

"Yes." The word slipped out, heedless of what it admitted and what it might lead to.

He lifted a hand to her cheek as though saluting her honesty. "Tonight then. If I stay here now, I'll want more of you and we have to stop. I don't have anything with me."

She looked her incomprehension.

"Protection." He stroked her cheek with seductive tenderness. His mouth tilted in a wry smile. "I trust you don't want to get pregnant."

"Oh!" A rush of blood to her head cleared the daze of stupidity. The realisation of what he was saying, what he was suggesting, stunned her anew. It was true. She might not have stopped him if he hadn't pulled back. But to assume she was willing to carry on with it tonight...did he only mean *know* in the biblical sense?

"I've been down that path," he explained soberly. "I won't risk it again. I got my son out of it but the marriage was hell."

She tore her mind off her own dilemma. It was important to hear what he was telling her, make sense of it, make sense of how it related to what they'd just experienced. The connection clicked loud and clear. No protection. A spontaneous sexual encounter...

"Your wife was pregnant when you married?"

"Yes."

It was being out of control that had appalled him. A hard lesson learnt? "Was that the only reason you married?" she asked.

He grimaced. "I couldn't bear the thought of my child being aborted."

"So you paid the price."

He nodded. "Though I did hope we could make a go of it. God knows I tried."

Logic, Angie thought, was amazingly easy to apply to something outside what she herself was feeling. His wife was in the past now. But the past cast a shadow, she reminded herself, even before he spoke the words that spelled it out to her.

"This...what we want from each other..." His eyes pierced her with his warning. "...Don't put a price on it, Angie. You'd better think about that. You can still change your mind. I'll respect whatever decision you make."

He tapped her cheek, stepped back, walked to the door, collected his hat from the peg, and left the schoolroom without a backward glance.

He'll get wet, she thought, then realised the rain had stopped.

The storm was over.

At least...the storm outside was.

CHAPTER SEVEN

TAYLOR'S mind bounced between wild exhilaration and cautious fear as he headed up to the house from the school. He'd never been turned on so fast and so far in his life as he had been just now with Angie Cordell! The night Hamish had been conceived, he and Trish had been partying for hours—too much to drink leading to stupid carelessness. With Angie... He shook his head...he had no explanation for almost losing all sense of where he was with her.

He wanted her, sure! He'd been thinking about it for a month. A lot of pent-up feeling there. With her, too. Maybe it was just the release of it that had made it so...so intense. Hell! He'd been on the verge of coming, just kissing her. And he ached from pulling back from it. He hadn't been in such a state since his teens.

Why, for God's sake? Was it the long drought of any sexual excitement in his marriage? One burst of it and he was like a boy again, driven beyond any common sense, impatient for more? It had been like spontaneous combustion. And he was still burning.

Tonight!

He half-groaned at the crassness of that suggestion. It was so damned bald, Angie would probably back off from it. Sheer physical need had blown his brain.

It was so long since he'd had good sex he was starved for it, but *tonight* was probably getting in too deep too soon with Angie. In more senses than one, he thought

77

with savage irony. Though it didn't change what he felt. Or what she felt, for that matter.

Could she handle the kind of straight deal he'd put to her? Some women preferred to let things happen rather than be faced with a definite decision. On the other hand, what point was there in pretending? The desire was mutual. No doubt about that. Why not be honest about it? He wanted honesty.

Which brought him up with a jolt, reminded of Angie's accusation he'd been less than honest in keeping things from her. It was true. Yet he hadn't really expected her to stay when he'd first brought her here. He'd been more or less waiting for her to concede it was the wrong place for her. He still wasn't sure it would prove right, despite her insistent arguments.

Nevertheless, he should have a word with his son. To Taylor's mind, there was a big difference between a negative attitude and downright nastiness. Dirty nastiness at that. The boy needed some straightening out. He'd talk to Thelma, too. Angie deserved a fair go from both of them.

He frowned over the other disturbing revelation arising from their conversation. If Trish had dished out physical abuse, he wanted to know about it. He hated the idea of Hamish keeping it to himself, suffering in silence, perhaps being threatened with more punishment if he told. It could explain the withdrawal into himself the past two years, the flashes of hostility.

He reached the veranda, took off his wet boots, then padded down the hallway to the kitchen in search of his son. Only Thelma and her two helpers were there. "Seen Hamish?" he asked, knowing the children would have come here to stuff their faces with cake or cookies after school.

"You'll probably find him in Leo's office," Thelma answered. "They went off together after the rain. Failing that..." She shrugged.

"Thanks."

Taylor nodded and left. The raising of sensitive issues with Thelma would best wait until after dinner when Yvonne and Gemma had gone.

He walked back down the hallway, past the staircase and opened the door to the office which was handily situated at the front of the house with glass doors to the veranda for easy access from outside. Leo and Hamish were both seated in front of the new computer, man and boy enthralled with its capabilities. They hadn't heard the door open.

Taylor paused, reflecting on what Angie had said about Leo fitting in and loving the life here. There was far more to it than using his computer skills. He'd quickly become a grandfather figure to Hamish, the two of them developing a very real bond of affection.

Trish had resented it but Taylor didn't, seeing it as a special relationship which their own families couldn't provide. Trish's parents lived in Brisbane and his were gone, his mother dying at thirty from breast cancer, undetected until it was too late to save her, his father losing his life in a flood ten years ago.

Leo was good with Hamish, always willing to give him time and lend a sympathetic ear to his needs and wants, obliging where he could. He'd won the boy's trust, something Taylor feared he had lost somewhere in the final mess of his marriage. If so, he needed to earn it again. He just didn't know how to reach past the wall his son had built around himself.

He closed the door, alerting them both to his intrusion.

They looked at him, Leo's expression openly enquiring, Hamish's closed and wary.

"Sorry to interrupt but I want to have a talk with Hamish. Would you mind leaving us for a while, Leo?"

"No problem." He turned to the boy. "Don't touch. We'll pick up on this later if you still want to."

"Okay," he sighed, his face reflecting reluctant resignation.

Once the older man had gone, Taylor took the chair he had vacated, wanting to establish a relaxed rapport. "So how's it going at school?" he asked lightly.

Eyes still wary. "Did you ask her?"

"Do you mean Angie?"

He nodded.

"I asked if she was managing okay."

"What did she say?"

"No problems. Said she found it all interesting. Do you like working with her, Hamish?"

He shrugged, relaxing a little, more assured now that Angie hadn't lodged any complaints about him. "She's not too bad," he said off-handedly.

"I've noticed you haven't been exactly friendly toward her. It's hard to come to a new place, not knowing anyone. Like when you go to Brisbane. It's easier if people are nice to you and make you feel welcome."

"That doesn't make you like it," he argued. "I don't like being in Brisbane."

"Do you think Angie doesn't like it here?"

He frowned. "I don't know. I thought she'd hate it. Like Mum. But she doesn't seem to," he added grudgingly, then more darkly. "Not yet, anyway."

"Why like Mum, Hamish?" Taylor asked quietly.

"She looks like her."

"No, she doesn't."

'She wears things like Mum. And she's pretty.''

''There's a lot of pretty women who wear fashionable clothes. Inside they're all different,'' Taylor explained, newly conscious of the truth Angie had spoken. ''Haven't you seen any differences, Hamish?''

''Maybe,'' he mumbled.

''There must be some,'' Taylor prompted.

''Well, she doesn't get mad at things,'' he slowly conceded. ''And you can tell she likes Jessie. She doesn't put her down or anything.''

Like Trish, he thought, who'd clung to a racist streak, despite all his arguing against it.

''And she doesn't send Wayne out, even when he acts up a bit.'' This evoked a rather smug smile. ''So he's stuck with doing his work. Like me. No getting out of it.''

''Sounds like Angie's doing a good job as your governess.''

''I guess.'' Another shrug.

''You shouldn't judge Angie by your mum, Hamish. It's not fair.''

''Guess not,'' he said uncomfortably.

''What did your mum do that you think Angie will do?'' Taylor pressed softly.

Hard accusing eyes. ''You know.''

''No, I don't.''

''She hit you, too. And screamed and yelled. I heard her.''

Dear God! He'd had no idea Hamish had been aware of Trish's tantrums. They'd gone on behind closed doors, mostly in their bedroom, well after he should have been asleep. There'd been the occasional bitter sniping from her in front of Hamish, but on the whole, Taylor had thought he'd kept their son reasonably shielded from the worst of it. Instead, he'd been subjected to it, too, obviously when Taylor wasn't around to stop it.

"Why didn't you tell me, Hamish?"

"You let her do it to you and you didn't do anything."

It wasn't the same! Yet what boy didn't try to be like his father, following the same code of behaviour? Taylor's heart bled for the child who'd tried to act like a man, faced with hysterical unreason and no clear path out of it.

"So you just took it and kept quiet," he murmured sympathetically.

Hamish nodded, his eyes full of the misery he'd kept to himself.

"I'm sorry, son. I didn't know she was like that with you. A man doesn't hit a woman, but I would have insisted she leave us and go back to Brisbane to live if I'd known she was hitting you."

"She would have made me go with her," he blurted out.

"I wouldn't have allowed it, Hamish."

"She said she would...and she tried to...the day she crashed the plane." Tears welled into his eyes. "She tried to make me go with her but I broke away from her and I ran and hid so she couldn't find me. She was yelling and screaming she'd get me from you anyway 'cause she was my mother."

"No..." It was more a groan than a denial.

The tears spilled over. "I'm glad she died," he said fiercely. "I wanted her to go and never come back. When she flew off I wished she'd just keep on flying to the other side of the world and get...get lost...and..." He choked. His face began to crumple.

And Taylor felt the guilt his son had carried this past

year, on top of all his stoic suffering, the fears and insecurity, and without a moment's hesitation, he reached out and lifted his child onto his lap, cuddling him close, rocking him and soothing him as a storm of tears gave release to some of the burden he'd carried.

"It's okay, son," Taylor murmured. "It's not wrong to feel that way when there's been so much hurt. But *you* didn't make her die, Hamish. It just happened. It could have been me in the plane. Or Gary. Whoever took it up that day would have crashed. None of us knew about the fault in the engine."

"But I got my wish," he sobbed.

"No, you didn't. You wished she'd fly to the other side of the world. You didn't wish the plane to crash," Taylor assured him. "You didn't really want your mum to die. You just wanted the bad things to stop."

Hamish bobbed his head.

Encouraged, Taylor went on, speaking feelings he himself had carried, the relief and guilt and grief of Trish's death. "You're glad the bad part is over, that's all. But Hamish, I know you're just as sad as I am that it ended with Mum dying. It would have been much better if we could have changed what was happening with all of us and made everything much happier for her. I'm sorry I couldn't do that for you, son. I just didn't know how…"

Irreconcilable differences. Everything he'd tried…the bargains he'd made…the compromises…all futile. There'd been no hope left at the end.

"It wasn't your fault, Hamish, Mum getting angry and hitting out. She was very unhappy inside herself. She needed help that we couldn't give her. She wasn't always like that…"

How far back did his son remember? When had the

abuse started? Two years...three? He was too distressed to be questioned. Taylor reasoned the more recent memories probably blotted out the better earlier ones.

"She got sick in her head, Hamish," Taylor tried to explain. "It was like all her thoughts and feelings got in a messy tangle and she couldn't unravel them. But in her heart she loved you. And I know in your heart, you loved her. She was your mum, no matter what. And you have to forgive the bad things because she didn't really mean to do them to you. She just couldn't help herself. She'd want you to remember the nice things about her. So try to do that, Hamish. It will make you feel better, too."

The sobs gradually quietened into the occasional hiccup. Hamish lifted a woebegone face from Taylor's damp shirt, his eyes still pleading for more reassurance. "Can Grandma and Grandpa Hayward take me away from you, Dad?"

So that was why he'd refused to go on every trip to Brisbane since Trish had died. It wasn't only the past that needed to be set to rest. The future held its bogeymen, as well.

"No, they can't, Hamish," he said firmly. "This is your home. Even if I died, this is your home with Thelma and Leo and everyone else who lives on this station. It will be your home as long as you want it to be."

"But you're not going to die, are you, Dad?" he asked anxiously.

"Not for a long time, I hope." He smiled to give his son confidence. "I expect to hang around until at least you take over the working of Giralang. If that's what you want to do."

A smile broke through. "Course I do. I'm going to be just like you."

"Hey now..." He tapped his son's chin. "Haven't I just finished telling you no two people are the same? I reckon you'll have to be a lot smarter than me at running this place with things changing all the time. I had to get Leo in to help me with the computer."

Hamish grinned. "Leo says I'm a natural at it."

"Well, there you go. Just don't get so wrapped up in computers you forget about people though." Taylor gave him a serious man-to-man look. "You know what it's like to be treated unfairly. Don't do it to others, son."

He sobered, a flicker of shame in his eyes. "You mean...like Angie."

"I mean everyone. Give them a fair go until you know for certain they're not worthy of it. Okay?"

"What if they turn out bad?"

"Then come and talk to me about it and we'll figure out how best to act. I guess you and I...we should have talked about Mum. I'm really sorry about that, Hamish. Is there anything else you want to ask about her?"

Encouraged to open up, Hamish sought relief from many secret worries and Taylor talked to his son for a long time, re-establishing confidence in their relationship, confidence and an assurance of love that could not be broken.

It occurred to him he had Angie to thank for ripping the scales off his eyes, forcing him to look beyond the surface of things. She was a very smart woman. He shouldn't forget she'd been hurt, too. As much as he wanted her, it ill behove him to ignore her emotional scars. Stupid to make simplistic assumptions. Above all, he had to be fair to her.

CHAPTER EIGHT

ANGIE lingered under the shower, hoping the beat of hot water would wash some of her physical tension away. In another forty minutes or so she'd be sitting down at the dinner table with Taylor Maguire. She had to have her mind sorted out before then. He'd be looking for signals from her.

Tonight…

Could she?

She wanted to…wanted to follow her instincts and believe it would all turn out right in the end, that the intimate sexual connection would lead to sharing all the other important areas, and they would find themselves in soul-warming harmony with each other. She wanted that to happen so badly…to have a truly good relationship, supportive of each other, caring, happy.

But getting in so deeply, right from the start, was a heart-on-the-line risk. How good was her judgment of any man, having made such a terrible mistake with Brian? In fact, might she not be feeling so strongly about Taylor because he belonged to what seemed like a solidly set permanence here at Giralang, a steady continuance that she found deeply attractive, almost compellingly so, given the lack of any secure roots in her life?

She saw no caprice in his character. She was certain he would stick to any commitment he gave. There was a very real sense of security in those two convictions. Yet there was no security about tonight. If she went his way, she would get the chance to really know him. If she backed off, would he pursue knowing her on other levels? He might interpret it as a lack of honesty on her part, a holding off to get more out of him. In which case, he would probably retreat to non-involvement and she would lose any chance of getting closer to him.

The last thing she wanted was to drive him away. She simply didn't know how far he would carry *respecting her decision*. She certainly didn't want *no* to mean *no* to everything between them.

Caution or blind trust…which was her enemy in this situation? What if Taylor only wanted sexual gratification? The sex between them might be wonderful but Angie knew she'd need more than that, and if nothing more was forthcoming…well, she could always leave. There was no contract between them. No commitment.

Don't put a price on it.

Taylor's warning played around her mind as she switched off the shower taps and proceeded to dry herself. He had scars from his marriage. *God knows I tried*—the words carried more than disillusionment, almost a helpless despair, indicating a deeper level of emotional scarring than she'd sustained from her relationship with Brian. The involvement of a child had to make anything bad even more damaging.

For all her arguments, the *city* tag would not be easily wiped from his mind. Harsh lessons left harsh imprints. After her experience with Brian, anyone wearing a *drug* tag wouldn't get easy entrance into her life. It was impossible to rely on them. Not to mention how scary it could all become.

She shuddered, the spectre of Brian's frightening disregard of her wishes still a close horror. So different from Taylor's, *I'll respect whatever decision you make.*

Taylor had treated her with respect all along. Even this afternoon she couldn't complain he hadn't listened to her. He'd been reasonable about everything. Except in kissing her. And that had gone beyond any reasonable expectation.

Attraction, desire, need...

Angie sighed as she drew on her silk wraparound, suddenly very conscious of her body and the loving it wanted. Loving, not just sex, she reminded herself, tying the belt tightly, trying to ward off temptation though it still persisted, tormenting her with its promises of pleasure and the fulfilment of hopes.

She walked quickly to the built-in cupboard in her bedroom and was in the process of choosing fresh clothes when there was a knock on her door. A firm knock. Her heart skipped several beats. He couldn't be coming to her now, she thought wildly, not before dinner. There wasn't time to...she blushed at the track her mind was taking, the track her body was wantonly responding to.

She moved into action to settle the issue, opening the door only wide enough to identify her visitor and hiding her state of undress behind it. Her head swam at the sight of Taylor, dominating the space so...so *physically*. His gaze instantly caught hers and held it, the blue eyes surprisingly warm and soft.

"I just wanted to thank you...for Hamish," he said, the deep timbre of his voice thrumming through her.

Angie was thrown into confusion. Taylor's son had completely slid from her mind. Yet the boy had to be important to him. More important than she was. She frowned, trying to get her wits in order. Taylor had not yet changed his clothes for dinner. He could have been talking to the boy. Her rather blunt appraisal of Hamish this afternoon might have had some effect.

"Would you like to explain that, Taylor?" she asked, sensing it was centred on things which had been kept from her.

He winced, his eyes darkening for a moment. "I guess I should. But for you…" A long, feeling sigh. "May I come in for a minute, Angie?"

A minute that could be critical to her understanding of this family. His mood would change if she said she wasn't properly dressed. The decision that caution was her enemy was instantaneous. However reckless it might be in the circumstances, she wanted—needed—to know what was on his mind. She pulled the door back to let him in and closed it after him to ensure privacy.

He'd taken only a few steps inside when she swung around. Any further movement was instantly arrested. He stared at her, his gaze fastening on the spill of curls from the rubber band she'd used to lift her hair on top of her head for her shower. Damp tendrils dangled around her face and neck and his attention was slowly drawn to them, dragging his gaze down, down to the thin silk wrap, wound revealingly around the nakedness underneath, the tightly tied belt adding emphasis to the full thrust of her breasts and the curve of her hips.

Angie hadn't imagined his preoccupation with his son would be obliterated so swiftly. She stood in helpless thrall to the intense focus on her, feeling the raw burst of desire building from it, her body reacting with a will of its own, her skin tingling, her nipples puckering into hard nubs, pushing against the silk, a hot moistness gathering between her thighs.

His head jerked a little as he wrenched his gaze up. Colour slashed across his cheekbones. His eyes wavered over hers. "I'm sorry. I didn't realise you were..." His hand lifted in an agitated gesture.

"I'd like to hear about Hamish," she blurted out, cutting through his embarrassment, anxious not to have him retreat. A deep breath. A visible reconcentration of his thoughts. Control regrasped. He nodded and moved away from her, crossing the room to the double glass doors that led out to the veranda. Angie had opened the curtains earlier. He stood looking out for several nerve-tearing moments. She saw his shoulders square. Then he half-turned, giving her face a long, searching look.

Angie had stayed by the door, incapable of any movement as her mind leapt through flaming hoops without getting anywhere. Impossible to discern *his* thought processes. All she knew was the wanting was even more alive than it had been this afternoon, as though having been sparked into tangible expression, it had caught fire and taken hold.

"Strange..." he said musingly "...if I'd brought home the governess I'd decided upon, instead of you, I'd probably be none the wiser about my son and what he's been feeling all this time. Before and after his mother's death."

Acutely aware of revelations hovering, Angie kept completely still, refraining from any prompting comment in case it deflected Taylor's train of thought.

"It was you...looking like Trish...and having the experience to be perceptive about children's behaviour."

Her restraint cracked, pain at his first observation driving her to rebut his words. "You said I didn't look like your wife."

He shook his head. "You don't. It's a certain style...class..."

The *city* tag!

"…And as Hamish put it…pretty." An ironic smile. "A boy's understatement. You are quite stunningly beautiful."

Her heart pumped chaotically, sending a tide of hot blood up her neck, flooding her cheeks with it. Brian had tossed such words at her. She had mostly dismissed them as glib flattery, ego-boosting at the time, pleasing to hear, yet not really real to her. She wanted them to be true from Taylor Maguire…at least, what *his* eyes saw, even though it wasn't true.

He expelled a deep sigh. "You were right about Hamish having been hit. I didn't know. Trish was…unstable…the last couple of years before she died. I thought it was centred on me but Hamish was also a focus of it."

Thelma knew, Angie thought. Or at least suspected it. Why hadn't Taylor's aunt spoken to him about it? Non-interference could be carried too far when a child was being abused. Though maybe if there was no escape route, interference could make matters worse. Sometimes there was no easy solution.

"Anyway, that's why you've been a target for hostility from him, Angie," Taylor said apologetically. "He's been carrying a lot of trauma around inside him. I hope it's been straightened out now. As well as it can be at this stage. He's not a bad kid…"

"I didn't say he was, Taylor," she put in quietly. "I think he'll be a fine boy, given the right direction and support."

"Yes."

For a moment she had a glimpse of the pride and love invested in his son. It touched her heart. She had no doubt he was a good, caring father, one who could be depended upon to do his best by his child. He must have been going through such hell with his wife and trying to keep it from his son, he'd probably been grateful for Hamish's withdrawal, not understanding what it meant.

Then he looked at her with an intoxicating blend of respect and admiration. "You're a good teacher, Angie."

Teacher—another tag.

"It is my profession," she reminded him dryly.

He shook his head. "You have a fine touch with children. It's a gift, not a job."

"Not so much a gift as knowledge and empathy," she corrected him, giving in to the urge to tell him about herself, wanting him to know more of the person beneath the tags he was placing on her. "I was hell on wheels to most of my teachers. When it comes to troubled kids, there's not much I didn't go through myself. It wasn't until my aunt got hold of me in my teens that I reformed and got direction. So I guess you could say I've been there. It gives me an advantage."

He frowned. "You did mention about your parents dying when you were young. I'd forgotten it."

"Not important to you. You'd already decided against me."

"Bad judgment." He gave her a conciliatory smile. "I can't thank you enough for steering me into drawing Hamish out. We settled a lot of bad stuff."

She smiled back. "Consider it a favour returned. You saved me from a lot of bad stuff."

For some reason the comment disturbed him. The tension, which had eased slightly, came screaming back. Angie saw his hand clench. He seemed to be struggling with some decision, not liking it, forcing himself into it. He shifted, facing her full-on, his expression set in de-

termination, yet his eyes warring with it as they fastened
on hers, probing with an urgent intensity.

"Angie...perhaps I was...impetuous...this afternoon."

His voice was strained and she could feel the rigid
restraint he was holding, the deliberate containment of
any show of desire for her. Her heart sank. If he was
intent on negating it, burying it, backtracking to his previous neutral position, he must have set his mind against
a close involvement with her, caution winning over
wanting.

"It hasn't been long since your...uh...unhappy entan-
glement with the guy in Brisbane," he went on, clearly
having difficulty in pushing his argument, given his earlier fervour for almost instant intimacy.

No...her mind screamed. He'd been there that last
night with Brian. He had to know there couldn't be a
shred of feeling left for a man who had persecuted her.
The affair was dead. Every bit as dead as his marriage
must have been at the end.

"It's been seven months since I finished with Brian,"
she stated flatly. "And it wasn't good before that. If
you're suggesting I might be on some rebound kick
where anybody else would look good to me, I'd take
that as an insult to my intelligence."

He looked pained.

He must want an out, Angie concluded, feeling sick
with disappointment. She dredged up the dignity to help
him end it gracefully. "If you want an excuse to put
distance between us again, Taylor, that one doesn't
wash. Why not simply be honest with me?" Her mouth
twisted with irony. "I'll respect your decision."

He stared at her. She could almost see the wavering
in his mind. Again his hands clenched as though re-

inforcing a control he found difficult to sustain. Angie fiercely willed it to break. They could have something good together. She felt it so strongly. If only he would let it happen.

"I don't feel right about taking advantage of...well, of your being here, employed by me," he said, the words tightly measured for serious impact.

Understanding swept in and almost buckled her knees with relief. A man of honour would hate the accusation of exploitation. He wanted free choice. She had to make him understand she did not view the situation as any kind of exploitation.

"I have a mind of my own, Taylor," she said quietly.

"Yes. Yes, of course you do." Relief. A wisp of a smile, both apologetic and appealing. "So what does your mind say, Angie?"

It didn't feel right to prevaricate. She'd made a firm stand. Her stomach contracted as the choice pulsed through her mind...caution or trust. It was a big choice. Yet, in a way, there was no choice at all.

"I want you," she said.

It was the truth, overriding everything else.

His mouth slowly widened into a smile of dazzling delight. "Honesty," he said, and laughed as he came toward her, released from restraint, his pleasure in her so evident, a cocktail of sheer joy fizzed through Angie.

Any sensible thought was beyond her. She simply feasted her eyes on him—this strong outback man who was beautiful to her—the embodiment of values and virtues that struck deep chords in her, important chords. Nothing else seemed to matter. She wanted, above all else, to share a sense of unity with him.

He stopped in front of her, and still smiling, reached out and tucked a stray curl behind her ear. "You are a remarkable woman, Angie Cordell,'' he said softly, his eyes simmering with his desire. ''Shall we pick this up after dinner?''

''If you want,'' she almost croaked, her throat having gone completely dry from the heat sweeping through her.

''I want.''

The murmured words had an intensity that seemed to thump into her heart, throb through her bloodstream. His fingertips trailed slowly down her throat, raising an exquisite sensitivity. They followed the edge of her wrap, nudging it aside, making room for the slide of his palm, skin against skin, hard flesh moving over soft, caressing the swell of her breast, travelling around it, under it, his thumb gently circling the aureole, teasing her nipple into more excitement.

Angie was totally mesmerised by the sensation of his touch, and all the time his eyes were locked on hers, sharing the mental intimacy of what he was doing, the silence between them heightening the flow of feeling. It was like doors being opened onto something entirely new, intensely seductive yet infinitely dangerous. This was the first step together, he leading, she willing, and soon there would be another step and another, and where they would go was impossible to tell, but retreat was no longer thinkable.

''I want to taste you,'' he said huskily. ''All through dinner, I'll be thinking of tasting you. I hope you'll be wanting to taste me, too.''

Then his hand was gone.

And he was gone.

And Angie was left to dress for dinner.

CHAPTER NINE

"ANGIE, would you mind serving the coffee in the TV room?" Thelma placed the tray on the table for Angie to take, and without waiting for her assent, shot a steely look at Taylor. "I'd like a word with you in the kitchen, Taylor."

Uncompromising demand. Thelma was on the warpath about something. "Sure!" he answered, quelling his impatience to have Angie to himself again. He rose from the dinner table, everyone else following suit.

"Great bread and butter pudding, Thelma!" Gary said appreciatively.

"Yes," Leo agreed. "Love those caramelised bananas, too."

"I'm sorry I was too full to eat much of it," Angie said ruefully, helping to collect the plates.

Thelma snorted at the excuse. "Watching your figure, no doubt," she remarked with a baleful look that swung from Angie to Taylor as she took the plates. She nodded at him, reinforcing the earlier demand, then marched off to the kitchen.

"I'll carry that tray for you, Angie," Gary said, swooping on it before she could demur. He grinned at her, taking away the sourness of Thelma's comment with his good humour.

She returned a smile. "Thanks, Gary."

He and Leo left for the TV room. Taylor stayed Angie from following, laying a hand lightly on her arm. He felt the slight tremor of nervous excitement and knew it had

96

robbed her of appetite. He'd felt the same way, forcing himself to eat the meal he was served while being totally unable to concentrate on it, his gaze continually straying to Angie's lovely face, the soft sensuality of her mouth, her golden-honey skin, the button-through orange dress that made his fingers itch to open it and free the delectable body it covered.

She lifted her gaze to his, the molten gold of her eyes swimming with vulnerability. "Thelma doesn't like me, Taylor," she murmured.

"She doesn't know you," he answered.

"Do you?" It was a searching challenge.

"Give me time. I won't be long with Thelma."

She sighed, offered him a wry smile, then pulled away, trailing after the others to perform the task allotted to her.

He watched her go; the cascade of curls around her shoulders, the seductive curve of her back, the sway of her hips. It was difficult to wrench his mind off the sheer allure of her femininity, but there was more than the physical to the attraction Angie Cordell exerted on him. Her challenge about knowing her raised his awareness of how few facts he actually did know about her life.

Somehow they didn't seem to matter. He liked the way her mind worked, the directness she applied to talking. There was no fluffing around with her. She made communication easy. He liked how she handled Hamish and the other children. He liked the quiet dignity with which she went about her life here, the respect she'd given to everyone on Giralang. He liked the person he had observed, the person she had shown him. It all added to his wanting her, fuel to the desire she'd stirred from the start.

He wanted the woman. All of her.

And she wanted him.

But he had to deal with Thelma first.

As he headed for the kitchen he reflected that he'd meant to talk to Thelma about her attitude to Angie. It was best done now. The bee in her bonnet needed its sting removed. He hoped his talk with Hamish would have positive results where Angie was concerned. God knew hostility was hard to live with. Who knew that better than he?

Angie had asked for a fair chance.

She had more than earned it.

Taylor smiled, thinking of the peaceful look on Hamish's face when he'd gone into his bedroom to say goodnight before coming down to dinner. The boy had already been asleep, emotional exhaustion probably taking its toll. At least his worries had been lifted. Tomorrow should be a happier day for him.

Thelma was at the sink, washing up, when he entered the kitchen. Taylor picked up a dish towel and joined her there. "What's the problem?" he asked, eyeing her grimly set face.

"You know perfectly well what the problem is, Taylor, and I'd advise you to put a stop to it before it's too late," she answered tersely. She paused in her washing to give him a meaning look. "You could have cut the air with a knife between you and Angie Cordell at dinner. I might be old but I can still see what's going on under my nose. And you can bet your boots Gary and Leo could, too. None of us are fools!"

"So?" Taylor tossed back non-committally.

Her eyes flashed furious frustration. "You want to make the same mistake again?"

"Angie isn't like Trish, Thelma," he stated coolly.

"And if you climbed down from your prejudice, you might see that for yourself."

"Prejudice!" she snorted and plunged her hands into the soapy water again, washing with unnecessary vigour. "I'm applying good old horse sense, Taylor. Once bitten, twice shy. If you want to sow oats, go to town. Getting into bed with Angie Cordell will only bring you grief."

"I don't think so."

She shook her head, agitated by what she clearly saw as madness. "You've only known her a month. At least give it more time."

"I don't want to."

Apart from his own urgent needs, it was now a matter of trust with Angie. He'd wanted honesty. He'd got it. What kind of man would he be to back off from her now?

Thelma slammed a plate into the dish rack and glared at him. "For God's sake! Think of the boy! You can't do this to him again, Taylor."

His heart contracted at the thought there'd been more abuse than he'd been told. "Do what, Thelma?" he asked quietly.

"Get into a relationship that will do him more harm. Trish tore that boy apart with her tantrums about leaving here and taking him with her. He used to sneak off as much as he could to keep out of her way. And he's doing the same with Angie Cordell."

Taylor breathed more easily. He picked up the plates in the rack and dried them as he answered his aunt. "I sorted that out with Hamish this afternoon. Like you, he was judging Angie on her appearance, not her character. I've made him understand how unfair that is," he added pointedly.

Thelma turned to him in exasperation. "The fact remains she is *not bred* to this life. Since you obviously feel the need for a woman, why in heaven's name, don't you pick on someone suitable? Someone who'll be a proper partner for you. It's not as if you're lacking in attraction. Diane Westlake is keen on you for one, and she'd fit in well here."

He grimaced. "Diane's a kid, Thelma."

"She's twenty-three. More than old enough for marriage in this country. Take another look at her."

"I've seen her recently enough."

She'd flown her father's plane in several times since Trish's death, supposedly neighbourly calls since the Westlake Station was only a hundred kilometres to the west of Giralang. He was aware she was sizing him up with future possibilities in mind, keeping it low key in respect for a mourning period. He hadn't wanted anything to do with a woman after Trish.

Until he'd met Angie.

"Diane Westlake would make you a good wife," Thelma muttered, banging some crockery together as she went back to washing.

Taylor gritted his teeth. "I'm not looking at marriage."

"You're just going to let Angie Cordell get her hooks in."

The jeering retort tightened his jaw further. "Angie's not like that."

"Every woman is like that with a man she wants."

"You're living in another era, Thelma."

"Human nature doesn't change."

"You're right!" he snapped, angered by the persistent blast of negativity. "I'm a man who's supposedly in his prime and I'd forgotten what it was like to be turned on by a woman. I've felt like a neuter for so damned long, it's like I've suddenly been given a new lease of life. So don't ask me to turn my back on it, Thelma. I'm human and I want to feel everything that being human entails. Including the pleasure of a woman I want.''

She swung to him, her face pained, her eyes anguished. "Taylor..."

"No! You've said enough! Too damned much, in fact. I'd be obliged if you'd keep your less-than-happy remarks about Angie to yourself from now on."

He tossed the dishcloth onto the workbench beside the sink and strode out of the kitchen, sick to death of *horse sense*. Maybe he *was* being a fool to plunge into an affair with Angie. He didn't damned well care! A man only had one lifetime. He was thirty-five years old and never before had he felt the high adrenalin charge Angie Cordell gave him. What's more, he might never feel it again. If he didn't follow it through he'd be a fool.

Besides which, he wasn't a total idiot. He planned to use protection. Angie understood the score. They were merely going to explore where this could go for them. Commitment could come later if they both wanted it. But nothing was going to stop him from seizing the moment and riding it for all it was worth.

He opened the door to the TV room and saw only Gary and Leo. "Where's Angie?" he asked, his sense of urgency heightened by the argument with Thelma.

"She didn't stay," Leo answered.

Gary grinned at him. "Wasn't interested in the program."

Taylor nodded and left, uncaring what they thought. He glanced in the lounge room, then the office on the off chance she had gone there to wait for him. Having drawn a blank, he took the stairs two at a time, his heart hammering, worried by the thought Angie might have sought the privacy of her bedroom for other reasons than wanting to be alone with him.

Her door was shut. No inviting crack of light to beckon him in. Taylor hesitated over knocking. Could she have had second thoughts because of Thelma's obvious disapproval? It didn't fit the strength of mind she'd shown. Though as her earlier challenge had pointed out, he didn't know everything about her.

All the same, he couldn't believe she'd shut him out without a word. The darkness had to mean she wasn't in her room. It was quite possible she'd gone for a walk. Physical exercise was always good for working off tension.

He moved on to his own room, striding through it to the door leading onto the veranda. From this upper level of the house, a scan of the immediate grounds might pick up where she was. He stepped out, catching a glimpse of her further down the veranda, standing by the railing, her face lifted to the stars.

He paused, struck by her air of aloneness. It raised a flurry of thoughts…no one for her to run to from that bastard in Brisbane. Parents long gone. What had happened to the aunt from her teens? Someone judgmental like Thelma?

Alone…cut off from her former life.

How much had it meant to her?

What did *he* mean to her?

Then she turned her head and looked his way, the slide of the door having penetrated her consciousness, or maybe simply sensing his presence. She didn't speak, didn't move, yet the concentration of her gaze on him was more arousing than any invitation.

Taylor forgot everything…except how much he wanted her.

CHAPTER TEN

SEEING him instantly dispelled Angie's sense of loneliness. The brightness of the stars was just as instantly forgotten. It was as though the whole universe didn't hold a candle to Taylor Maguire. He walked toward her, a warm living force, a magnet she couldn't resist, a field of energy that inexorably drew on hers, fueling feelings she was powerless to control.

The emotions that had been churning through her—fear of the unknown, rage against fate for delivering her into yet another set of difficult circumstances, sadness over the misery inflicted through conflicts of interest—suddenly seemed superfluous, ephemeral, meaningless things. This man was a basic, vital reality, impossible to ignore or set aside.

She felt every part of her springing with excitement as he closed the dark distance between them, looming nearer and nearer, filling her vision, his face a tantalising mixture of shadow and light, the glow of his eyes an unwavering constant, transmitting a need that would not be denied.

He reached her and with barely a pause, took her hand and slowly lifted it, carrying it to his lips. He held her gaze with hypnotic intensity as he kissed her palm, tasted it, his tongue moving down her lifelines as though probing them for intimate knowledge, then sweeping the softer, fleshier pad at the base of her thumb. It gave her the most extraordinary sensation, as though her hand was a precious receptacle and he was pouring his life essence into it, through it, infiltrating her entire body with it.

Drawn to seek more of him, she turned to lift her other hand to his face, touching the hard, smooth planes of it, her fingers grazing over his skin, wanting to feel the man inside, needing to reach into him as deeply as he was reaching into her. She felt a muscle in his jaw contract, a reaction, a response to her instinctive quest. His eyes suddenly blazed with a searing hunger.

"Yes…" The word exploded from his lips as he lowered her palm, pressing it over the thumping beat of his heart. "I can't bear it. I can't bear it any longer." Raw words, cracking through long-held self-containment. "Come with me."

He captured her other hand and pulled her after him along the veranda, and the night pulsed with danger as she followed in his footsteps, his urgency tearing through her, compelling her on. His door was still open. He took her into the dark cavern of his bedroom and the throb of secret privacies kicked through Angie's heart, the fear of unleashed sexuality beating through the powerful promise of more revelations.

"Touch me now," he commanded, drawing her hands to the hot breadth of his chest, already bare, his shirt unbuttoned and pulled apart. "Touch me wherever you want."

She responded more to the desperate longing in his voice than her own desire, though both drew her into pleasuring him as he directed…blindly, in the ink-blackness of the room, stroking, softly exploring, suddenly revelling in the strange intimacy of it. His flesh felt so alive, rippling with muscles as he dragged off his shirt. Her fingers found his nipples and teased them as he'd teased hers, exulting in her power to excite when she heard him groan.

Her nerves leapt at the snap of the waist stud on his jeans, the rip of his zipper. Her mind registered the point of no return but she couldn't stop touching him, the bunched muscles in his shoulders as he bent to pull off the rest of his clothes, the cords running up his neck, the sheer maleness of his back.

Then he was standing upright again and she knew he was completely naked now, knew he was wholly accessible to her touch, vulnerable to it, and the power he was giving her was intensely moving and daunting. It was the power to hurt, to reject, and it implied a level of trust that squeezed her heart.

The barriers were gone, discarded, and the challenge of acceptance was placed upon her. Her response would measure her wanting for him. No lies. No deception. Naked truth. Primitive, but oh so tangible evidence of her desire to take this journey with him.

Rightly or wrongly, it made Angie feel incredibly special, and her fingers tingled with tenderness as she caressed him, caring for him, wanting him to know and feel he was special to her. Because he was. And this first time would never come again and what she did now was important. It was sexual. It was erotic. It was also an act of love, of giving what was needed and wanted, of reaching out and touching on the most basic terms of all.

He unbuttoned her dress. In a strange way it was like a ceremony, the slow peeling away of her clothes, the touching, the thrall of being exquisitely sensitised, his hands so seductively gentle on her, erotically knowing yet unhurried, savouring every part of her, revelling in every quiver of response. The only sound was their breathing and the darkness added mystery, heightening the sense of discovery, banishing any shame, focusing everything on touch and feeling.

Her mind blurred between fantasy and reality. She lost all sense of past and future. This wasn't so much Taylor and Angie, but man and woman meeting in a time and space that had nothing to do with anything else. It was as though this was a beginning in a world which was yet to know the light of day, the birth of a new life, stirring into consciousness, becoming more and more aware, the fascination of searching, the awe of finding, the sweet satisfaction of knowing.

And when he drew her against him and kissed her, the escalation of feeling was so intense, she needed the lock of his arms around her to hold it in, needed the support of his body as he moved her with him. He lowered her onto a bed and she lay there in helpless abandonment to the kisses he rained on her, spreading rivulets of heat through her as he tasted all he wanted to taste, shaping her breasts to his mouth, piercing her with pleasure as he sucked on them, his hands stroking her stomach, parting her legs, his lips trailing hotly, sensually after them, his tongue circling her navel, circling down, down, finding the folds of her sex, nudging them aside, probing until he found what he wanted, what she was dying for him to find, and he was kissing her there, and she couldn't stop herself from thrusting at him softly, achingly hungry for the ultimate fulfilment of the need screaming through every nerve now.

He went on and on, seemingly exulting in the taste of her womanhood, revelling in the freedom to satisfy his hunger for it, sending sharp, leaping streaks of desire through her, the pleasure of it unfurling, driving her toward climax. She felt the circling tide growing, felt the melting start, and she didn't want it like this, not with him outside her, not sharing in it. She writhed away from him, crying out, "No, please. I want you with me."

She heaved herself up to pull at him, to bring him over her, needing to feel all of him joining with her. She'd forgotten protection but he hadn't. He deftly applied it then settled on her very gently, calming her, holding her poised on the edge of anticipation as he guided himself on the inward journey she craved.

"Be still now! Be still," he commanded, his voice strained with the effort to control, and she knew he didn't want it to be over quickly, knew he didn't want any moment of this experience with her to escape him, knew he'd been holding himself back to ensure he missed nothing.

She tried to hold still, concentrating fiercely on the feel of him as he entered her, but it was so slowly her muscles convulsed around him, begging for more, drawing on him, urgent and insistent and needful. He pushed further, filling her, filling her beautifully, exquisitely, as he went on and on, sliding carefully. She curved and grew around him, making way, welcoming, feeling him become part of her, she part of him as he gradually sank all of himself into her.

There he remained long enough to kiss her, taking her mouth with his so tenderly Angie almost wept from the sheer emotion of it, the deep togetherness it reinforced, the caring in the knowing of it, the welling of pleasure in the sharing, the bonding of their bodies into one.

Then he moved, moving her with him as he worked a rhythm that revelled in discovery, pushing new boundaries, reaching for more and more sensation, driving, thrusting, a wild friction of heat, of pulsing flesh, spreading inwards and outwards, building great fronds of pleasure that bloomed with spangles and sunbursts, invading her arms and legs. She felt her strength ebbing, felt suspended in helplessness as he came into her harder, faster, stronger, and she climbed higher and higher with each beat, until the beat turned into rolls of sweet chaos and she yielded everything up to him as she floated on waves of ecstatic wonder.

Then she felt him come, too, the deep long throbbing of him, the spasms of release, heard his groan at the ultimate expenditure of self and his sigh in the triumphant satisfaction of it. She opened her eyes and looked at him as he lifted himself up from her, saw the solid silhouette of his head thrown back, raised upward, and sensed the sheer glory of their coming together running through him. When he sank down beside her, he gathered up her limp body, nestling it against his, her head on his shoulder, and he kissed her hair and cradled her close, making her feel valued and cherished.

Neither of them spoke. Somehow the silence kept all they had felt safely cocooned, and the darkness provided a comforting blanket, preserving the warmth and the intimacy. But it was only physical intimacy, and however much Angie told herself it couldn't have been a better start to their relationship, she wanted to know how much weight it carried in Taylor's mind. Indeed, whether it was all that *was* on his mind.

She had never been made love to so thoroughly. Nor so intensely. The experience was incomparable to anything she had shared with Brian, on an entirely different plane. And it hadn't come from her. It had been *drawn* from her by Taylor, the initiatives he had taken, the mood he had set, the feeling pouring from him.

Why? she wondered. Why had he brought her to his room when hers had been so much closer? Perhaps his own territory had made him feel more in control, yet he had more or less ceded control to her in many ways. It suddenly occurred to her they were lying on the bed he had shared with his wife. It was a disquieting thought. Was all of this part of some drive to exorcise memories of his marriage? Bad memories? What had gone on—or not gone on—in this bed with his wife?

"Thank you."

The soft murmur was barely a puff of breath through her hair, yet it instantly touched Angie's train of thought, stirring her to ask, "What for?"

"For being you." She could hear the smile in his voice, felt his deep satisfaction, but it didn't tell her anything she didn't know.

"Would you like to explain that in terms I can pin down a bit?" she lightly invited.

He laughed, a rich rumble of pleasure. Then he shifted, easing her onto her back as he propped himself up on his elbow. He gently stroked her face, raking the tumbled curls away from it. "You came with me all the way." His tone carried a soft lilt of surprise mixed with warm appreciation. "No questioning. No baulking at anything. Not even a hesitation. Not once did I feel you weren't in tune with me."

Angie frowned over his answer. Did he think she would go to bed with someone she didn't feel in tune with? What point would there be in it? "I did say I wanted you, Taylor," she softly reminded him.

"Yes. But there are many shades of wanting. And many motives behind it."

"You were...testing me?" She recoiled from the idea even as she expressed it.

He shook his head. "I was being totally selfish, doing whatever I wanted."

She laughed, relieved and amused by his claim.

"You're not a selfish lover. Believe me, I know what that's like." She thought of many nights with Brian when she had lain awake, unsatisfied, after he had taken his pleasure and fallen asleep.

"Have you had many lovers?" he asked curiously, no hint of judgment in his voice.

"No. Only two. One in my rebellious teen years. Then no one else until Brian. Whom I thought was all I wanted in a man," she added with bitter irony.

He trailed his hand down her throat and made idly erotic circles around her breasts, spreading tingles of excitement again. "I can understand why he didn't want to lose you," he murmured, as though her body answered everything he wanted.

Angie was impelled to a fierce rebuttal. "Then he shouldn't have lied to me. Nor spun out on drugs. Nor rolled into bed with someone else. Maybe I ought to know where you stand on that, Taylor."

"I don't like living with lies." He leaned over and licked one nipple into instant hardness. "Nor have I any need or desire for an artificial high on drugs." He treated the other to the same delicate teasing. "And I remained faithful to Trish throughout our marriage."

It was reassuring to have her judgment affirmed. A commitment, once given by this man, would be honoured. He wasn't looking for easy escapes, not with lies nor with drugs. It simply wasn't in his character. Maybe outback people learnt to ride out the blows of fortune, enduring whatever had to be endured until better times came.

"In fact..." He lifted his head, coming back to his propped position. "...You are the only woman I've been with since Trish." His fingers grazed tantalisingly over her stomach. "The only woman I've wanted to be with."

Angie took it as a compliment and was comforted by it, reassured he wasn't the kind of man who would ever take a woman lightly.

He leaned over and brushed her mouth with his, a soft, sensual kiss, through which he breathed the words, "Stay here. I'll be back in a minute."

Then he rolled away from her, off the bed, and she heard him stride quickly to the other end of the room, open a door, close it. An ensuite bathroom, she assumed, imagining him removing the protective sheath, perhaps getting another, hungry for more sex.

She frowned over that thought, yet it did answer what she'd felt coming from him, and if he'd been celibate for so long… *I can't bear it! I can't bear it any longer!* The words he'd spoken suddenly jangled in her mind like warning bells she should have heeded. If Taylor had simply used her, a willing woman, readily available… Angie couldn't bear it!

She frantically fumbled through the dark for a bedside lamp and found one, switching it on to spread some light on what she needed to know. Darkness might have been the cloak for playing out a sexual fantasy. She needed to see Taylor's face when he came back and she wanted him to see hers. It had to be stamped on his consciousness that she was a real person, as vulnerable to hurt as anyone else.

Agitated by a flood of doubts, she shot her gaze around the room he'd brought her to. No photographs of his wife anywhere. No feminine touches left in place. She was on a king-size bed and the rest of the furniture and furnishings were suited to a male taste, shades of blue and brown, heavy-duty chairs and chest of drawers.

Her pounding heart contracted painfully as the door he'd used was opened. Her breath caught in her throat as Taylor stepped into the bedroom and paused, registering the effect of light, staring at the vision of her sitting upright in his bed. She hadn't thought to cover herself—didn't think now.

The sight of him stunned her into mindless admiration for several moments. Seeing him naked was different to feeling him naked. He had the kind of physique sculpted by Michelangelo, beautifully male, perfectly proportioned, but no way could he be mistaken for a cold work of art. His skin glistened with the heat of life and his body exuded such a powerful energy, Angie was swamped by desire again.

"Was it time…or me, Taylor?" she blurted out, driven to ask before he came to her.

He frowned, lost on the context of the question.

"You had a long, celibate period," she reminded him.

His brow cleared. His eyes glowed at her. "It's you. How can you doubt it?" He shook his head as though she amazed him. "I have had offers, Angie. I just didn't want to take them up. Not enough, anyway."

So she *was* special. Even if it was only in the strength of sexual attraction, she had reached something in him others hadn't. The pressure on her heart lifted and her head almost dizzied with pleasure as he grinned at her.

"I'm glad you turned on the light," he said, moving back to the bed and sprawling across it. He picked up her foot and began playing with her toes, a warm happy twinkle in his eyes. "Now I can have the pleasure of watching you, too."

Angie gave up worrying.

The darkness was gone and this was real enough for her.

To begin with.

CHAPTER ELEVEN

THE plane flew in as Angie and the children were strolling back to the schoolroom after morning tea.

"Westlake's Cessna," Hamish said, identifying it as a familiar visitor to Giralang.

He'd been quite talkative all morning, actually smiling at Angie when she praised his work. Credit for his more favourable disposition toward her probably had to be given to Taylor's straightening-out talk with him yesterday. Nevertheless, she couldn't help feeling pleased. It made everything so much easier with Taylor if his son could like her. Especially after last night.

"Bet it's Diane Westlake coming to see your dad again," Wayne tossed at Hamish, his dark eyes sparkling with mischievous teasing.

Hamish threw him a dirty look. The jut of his chin and tightly clamped mouth denied any further rising to the bait.

Angie was puzzled by his truculence. The two boys usually swapped banter with easy good humour, neither taking offence. Since she knew nothing about the woman mentioned, she had no idea of the purpose for this visit, but Hamish's attitude certainly raised questions. He either didn't like the woman or didn't like her talking to his father.

Jessie, always eager to be helpful, turned a knowing smile to Angie. "My mum reckons Diane Westlake is sweet on Hamish's dad."

"Shut up, Jessie!" Hamish shot at her fiercely.

113

A sense of unease crawled down Angie's spine.

Unabashed, Jessie adopted the superior air of an older girl who knew better than her younger male companions and proceeded to shoot Hamish down. "Then why do you think she's been turning up here so much since your mum died?"

"Yeah...sticking her nose in," Wayne piped up again, jumping on the bandwagon.

"It would join up the two biggest cattle stations in the gulf if they got married," Jessie said importantly.

It was clear to Angie this was a repetition of common gossip and she didn't like it any better than Hamish did.

He rounded on Jessie, blue eyes blazing. "My dad's not going to get married. Ever again," he cried vehemently.

Jessie planted her hands on her hips and defied him. "Did *he* tell you that?"

"You just shut up, Jessie Gates."

"See?" she jeered. "*You* don't know."

"That's enough, Jessie," Angie cut in firmly. "You don't know, either, and it's none of your business anyway." She forced an appealing smile. "Let's drop it, shall we?"

Jessie huffed, crestfallen at having been rebuked. Wayne shoved his hands in his pockets and whistled at the sky. Hamish kicked up gravel from the drive as he walked on, head lowered in dark brooding.

Angie had much food for thought herself and she didn't like any of it. While she accepted there were no promises attached to this affair with Taylor, the intimacies and confidences of last night had led her to believe there was a good chance of forging the kind of relationship she'd dreamed about, with a firm foundation of understanding between them, a sharing of values, and the deep feelings aroused and cemented by their instinctive and strong desire for each other. Was she hopelessly fooling herself? Did Taylor just want his bed warmed while he considered a future with Diane Westlake?

Her buoyant spirits punctured, Angie found it difficult to concentrate on supervising the children's work over the next two sessions. Fortunately, the school of the air schedule had Jessie's class on first, Year 5 Library, and she didn't need help. The boys settled quietly into their story-writing, though Angie noticed Hamish's pen didn't move much. He was clearly disturbed.

Certainly the idea of having a stepmother didn't appeal to him, which was understandable, having suffered abuse from his natural mother. However, he might very well view any woman who got close to Taylor as a threat he didn't want to live with. In which case, Angie's position as his governess would quickly become untenable if her closeness to Taylor continued as she wanted it to, and it couldn't stay completely hidden for long, no matter how discreet they were.

She had hoped to establish a comfortable rapport with the boy, given time. With this in mind, she had agreed with Taylor on sensible discretion with their relationship, since Hamish had yet to learn to like her and no good could come out of shaking his newly built sense of security. Now, however, Angie found herself fighting with the suspicion that Taylor might have more motives for discretion.

Did Diane Westlake play a part in his thinking?

Obviously *she* didn't wear a city tag and at least some of the people on Giralang saw an advantageous match in the making if Taylor was inclined that way. Angie tried to reassure herself with Taylor's claim he hadn't wanted any of the women on offer. But maybe Diane

Westlake hadn't offered herself yet, respecting a normal
period of mourning while indicating a personal interest
if he wanted to pursue it when he was ready.

It would surely be in his mind to make a sensible
marriage next time. *If* there was to be a next time.
Commonality of purpose, a shared lifestyle with no conflicts over it, the natural understanding that came from
the same background and upbringing…such factors had
to have a positive impact on him where a long-term relationship was concerned. He was certainly wary of sex
leading him into marriage. No matter how aroused he
was, he was meticulous about protection.

Not that Angie could fault him on it. She certainly
didn't want an unplanned pregnancy. Nor had marriage
been on her mind. She wouldn't even begin to consider
a long future with Taylor at this stage, when so much
could go wrong. Brian had taught her a salutory lesson
on that score. She would have married him if he'd asked
her early on in their relationship and it would have been
a huge mistake.

She just wished she had known about Diane Westlake
yesterday. The woman might not be important to Taylor
at all, but her arrival today certainly pointed up problems
Angie hadn't thought through last night. This wasn't the
city where a man and a woman could pursue their in-
clinations without affecting others. This was a tightly
knit world where Taylor's business probably was everyone else's business.

Jessie's library session finished. It was followed by a
general scripture lesson, listened to by all three children.
Angie's mind kept drifting off it, fretting over Diane
Westlake's visit to Giralang. Did it mean her staying
overnight? For several days? Was such extended hospitality taken for granted in the outback? Surely some-

one would have spoken about her coming if she had been expected. On the other hand, perhaps she knew she was always welcome.

The lunchbreak came. Wayne and Jessie skipped ahead as they trooped up to the house. Hamish was in no hurry. He walked beside Angie, a closed, belligerent look on his face. She didn't try to talk to him. For once, she was in complete sympathy with his feelings. Their visitor was no more welcome to her as she was to him. It gave them some mutual ground, not that Hamish was aware of it.

Yvonne and Gemma were already handing Jessie and Wayne their share of a pile of roast beef sandwiches when Angie and Hamish arrived in the kitchen. Thelma, probably drawn by their chatter, appeared in the doorway to the dining room.

"Come and say hello to Diane, Hamish," she instructed, encouraging him with a benevolent smile. Her eyes were not so warm when she lifted them to Angie but they weren't quite as frosty as usual. "Would you come, too, Angie? The Westlakes are our closest neighbours and Diane would like to meet you. We'd be pleased if you joined us for lunch."

"That's very kind. Thank you."

Neatly trapped for a woman-to-woman appraisal, Angie thought, suspecting Diane had already been given an earful about her from Thelma. There was no doubting whose side Taylor's aunt would be on if a rivalry for his affections was underway. Hamish, however, hung back beside Angie in the meeting that followed, using her as a buffer against any advance on his space by Diane Westlake.

After the formal introduction was politely negotiated, Angie had time to study the younger woman as she tried

to engage Hamish in friendly conversation. She *was*
younger, early twenties, Angie judged, with an appealing
girl-next-door look, no obvious artifice about her. She
was naturally pretty, regular features, dark blond hair cut
to a short bob, very attractive green eyes.

Her slender figure was sensibly attired in dark blue
jeans and a multicoloured check shirt, giving her a
down-to-earth look. The shirt, however, was not *country*—Angie's practised eyes recognised designer label—
but it would look *country* to a man. Angie made a private bet it wasn't worn to work in. It was worn to be
eye-catching and bring out the green in her eyes.

What struck her most was Diane's air of confidence.
Age was irrelevant. This woman knew who she was and
her place in the world. If there was such a thing as
landed gentry in Australia, Diane Westlake belonged to
it, born and bred to it, just like Taylor. She was also
very much at home at Giralang, betraying none of the
uncertainties a sometime guest might have. Angie envied
her that. More than ever before, she felt like an outsider
looking in on a privileged circle, wanting to be part of
it, knowing she wasn't.

After a series of monosyllabic replies from Hamish,
Diane graciously let him go to spend the lunch hour with
the other children. Then it was Angie's turn to be subjected to questions, couched in a getting-to-know-you
format, but the bottom line was very similar to that in
the interview with Taylor at the Brisbane Hilton... Why
would a city woman, a professional teacher, want to be
an outback governess?

Angie doggedly ate her portion of shepherd's pie in
between giving answers and sliding in her own questions. Nothing of a deeply personal nature was said by
either party. Diane had gone to a boarding school in

Brisbane for her senior school years—Angie knew it to be a very expensive one—then on to agricultural college before picking up her life on the home station again. Having a Cessna plane at her disposal was probably better than a sports car, Angie thought.

"Everyone on the radio line is very curious about you," Diane commented with a charmingly disarming smile. "Why don't you join in the chat sessions each morning?"

Angie returned a rueful smile. "I don't know the people."

"Oh, no one waits on ceremony up here. You just introduce yourself and natter on."

"It seems...presumptuous. I prefer to meet people first." Having been warned of the gossip mill by Taylor, she was not about to feed it, especially not knowing whom she should be wary of.

"Well, you'll be meeting them all at the picnic races but that's three months off. It's a great occasion, isn't it, Thelma?"

A glow of approval from Taylor's aunt. "Diane and her family organise it all. The picnic races are held at their station each year and everyone flies in for the event. Even some city friends come for it," she added meaningly. "Perhaps there's someone you'd like to invite, Angie."

She deflected the probe for information with another smile. "Thank you for telling me."

"In the meantime, getting on the radio could help you find your feet amongst our widespread community," Diane suggested.

Angie shrugged it off. "I guess I'm used to finding my own feet." Her face was aching from smiling.

"But everything must be so strange to you out here," Diane pressed.

"I like learning. Speaking of which, it's time to collect the children for the afternoon lessons."

Angie was grateful for the excuse to get away, feeling she'd been pecked at all through lunch. Perhaps it was her own sense of insecurity colouring everything said, but Diane's facade of friendliness had seemed false to her, false and threatening. There was purpose in this visit all right, and it had nothing to do with trying to help an outsider find her feet in the outback world. Angie could only await developments for the picture to become clearer. Meanwhile, treading carefully seemed her best option.

Hamish looked as miserable as Angie felt when they settled back in the schoolroom. The three children worked on their mathematics sets for the forty minutes, with Angie checking their progress in case they needed help. Wayne claimed most of her attention. He was always restless after lunch. Once the sets were completed, Angie decided to put on one of the Human Resources and Environment videos, which was both entertaining and educational, an easy way to finish off what had turned into a stressful day.

Diane dropped in just as the video ended. "Hi! Hope I'm not interrupting anything important." She cast a bright look around the children who were obviously not hard at work. "Thelma tells me Taylor and Gary are fixing a leaking bore. Number twelve, which is only about seven kilometres away. Want to ride out with me, Angie?"

Much as she would have liked to observe Taylor and Diane together, Angie knew instinctively the other woman meant to put her at a disadvantage. "It's kind of you to ask, but..."

"Oh, the kids can have an early mark for once," she cut in, assuming an authority she had no right to.

"Yeah!" Wayne cheered.

"And I'm sure Gary would enjoy having your company," Diane went on.

The deliberate pairing off of couples put Angie in her place—the underling who could be manoeuvred anyhow Diane wanted. Angie inwardly bristled. She was sorely tempted to say the man she'd slept with last night might prefer to be partnered with her, but she held her tongue. Jolting Diane's overweening confidence would be a hollow victory if it put Hamish offside with her. Besides, it was up to Taylor to spell out where they stood with him.

She forced another aching smile and said, "No, thank you. I'm not really comfortable on a horse yet."

"Oh! Pity!" An apologetic grimace. "I forgot you weren't born in the saddle like the rest of us."

Like hell she had!

The grimace widened to a sweet smile. "I'll see you later then."

The moment the door closed behind her, Wayne started agitating for an early mark anyway. Too depressed to pour out positive energy in a discussion of the video, Angie agreed. He and Jessie whooped happily and shot outside but Hamish stayed in his seat, his gaze fixed intently on Angie.

"Is something wrong, Hamish?" she asked.

"I've seen you riding with Joe," he blurted out, almost accusingly.

"Then you must know I'm still a learner."

"You could have gone with her to see Dad."

It was clear he didn't like the idea of Diane being alone with his father, even though Gary would be there, as well. Angie surmised he saw her more as a possible spoke in the other woman's wheel than someone he'd prefer his father to be with.

"I think Diane meant to gallop, Hamish," she said dryly. "I wouldn't be any good to anyone if I fell off and hurt myself. It would only cause trouble."

He frowned, seeing the sense in her explanation, yet still disliking the situation. Several minutes passed as he pondered the problem. Angie waited patiently, knowing nothing would be gained by hurrying him. The boy had to sort out his own feelings, though she found it interesting and encouraging that some basic trust in her was emerging.

"I reckon you could handle a ride to the river," he said at last. "We could go slow." His blue eyes were suddenly full of adult responsibility. "I'll look after you, Angie. You won't fall with me. I'll ride alongside and take you the safest way."

Her heart leapt at the offer. Whatever Hamish's reasons for it, this was the first crack in his reserve toward her and a chance for Angie to reach out to him on a more personal level. "Thank you, Hamish. I'd really appreciate that," she said warmly.

He grinned, pleased at her agreeing to his plan. "I'll ask Joe to saddle your horse while you get ready to go."

"You mean right now?"

"Sure. Why not? I'll show you all the good spots at the river," he pressed, eagerly rising to his feet.

It had to be more a gesture against Diane than toward her, Angie reasoned, but she was not about to knock back an opportunity to make progress with him. "Okay.

I'll grab some cookies on my way through the kitchen,'' she offered supportively.

"Great!"

They left the schoolroom together, good humour restored as they hurried off to carry through their arrangements. Angie reflected that her riding with Hamish might be seen as a snub of Diane's prior invitation but there was quite a difference in the distances, the river being only three kilometres away. Besides, earning favour with Hamish was more important to her life here with Taylor than travelling in Diane Westlake's dust.

As for the man himself...

Angie's chest tightened.

She hoped she wasn't making a huge mistake with Taylor Maguire. If by word or deed he denied the attraction between them in front of Diane Westlake...well, it was probably better to be hurt sooner rather than later.

CHAPTER TWELVE

IT WAS quite beautiful by the river. In contrast to the vast plains stretching into seemingly endless distance away from it, the area close to the water was heavily treed, providing pleasant shade from the heat. The rocky banks sloped so gradually, pools were captured in them, favourite places for the local wildlife. Hamish pointed out a tortoise and a water lizard, as well as identifying all the birds they saw.

True to his promise, he'd watched over Angie's handling of her horse on the way out and tethered both horses to a low-hanging branch while he took her for a walk along the river, adopting the role of teacher as he pointed out the many interesting facets of their environment. Angie couldn't fault him as a companion and she was impressed with his knowledge which he accepted as perfectly natural. This was his world and he loved it.

Eventually they sat on a boulder to rest and Angie risked one small probe into his private thoughts. "Thank you for sharing this with me, Hamish. I've been wanting to come out here."

He picked up a stone and lobbed it into the water, watching the ripples from its entry before answering her. "There's a good place for catching fish further up," he said. "I'll show you another day."

"I'd like that."

He nodded, offering nothing more.

After a few silent minutes, Angie glanced at her

watch. "I guess we ought to be starting back. It's almost five o'clock."

"*She'll* be there," he muttered, bending to pick up another stone. It was more an angry toss this time.

"Why don't you like Diane, Hamish?" Angie asked quietly.

He slanted her a knowing look. "You don't like her, either."

Angie couldn't deny it.

"Mum said she was like a crocodile."

It was his first mention of his mother. Angie kept her mouth shut, wary of making a wrong comment.

"I heard her telling Dad," he went on. "Yelling it at him."

"Maybe she didn't mean it," Angie said softly.

He flashed her a dark look. "It's true. Mum said she was lying on the bank waiting for Dad and when she had him in her sights, she'd slide in and gobble him up."

Angie couldn't help thinking it was an apt description of Diane Westlake, but she felt Hamish wanted his fears diminished. "I don't think your father is the kind of man who'd get taken by a crocodile. Doesn't he watch out for them?"

"Yes. But she keeps coming," he added uncertainly. "Like it's her territory."

"Well, maybe your father lets her come because he knows she hasn't got any teeth."

He looked at her, startled for a moment, then broke into a laugh. "She has so got teeth, Angie," he corrected her in very boyish amusement.

"But maybe not ones capable of gobbling him up."

He grinned at her, relieved by this point of view. Angie could only hope it was true, as far as Taylor was concerned.

"Hamish… Angie…"

Their names boomed off the river, instantly turning their heads to the direction of the caller.

"We're just around the bend, Dad," Hamish yelled back.

Angie leapt up from the boulder, surprised that Taylor had followed them here. With Diane?

The clatter of hooves on stones heralded a fast approach. He came into view, seated on a big black horse which he pulled to a halt once he saw Angie and Hamish standing together. His gaze fastened on Angie, quickly scanning her from head to toe. "You're all right?" he asked, as though wanting her reassurance it was so.

"Course she is, Dad," Hamish answered for her. "I've been looking after her."

He looked at his son and his face relaxed into a smile. "That's good, Hamish. Angie is still a bit nervous about riding. I wasn't sure you knew that."

He'd come to check on her. Never mind what Diane had wanted. Angie felt the smile blooming inside her before it burst across her face. "I wasn't nervous coming here. Hamish rode beside me and kept watch all the time."

"Well, accidents can happen," Taylor remarked, his initial tension dissipating as he dismounted with a fluid grace Angie admired and envied. Maybe she could match that someday. Match him in every way.

"Angie's not silly, Dad," Hamish informed him.

It evoked a grin that set Angie's heart pumping overtime. "No, she's not. In fact, she's probably the smartest lady I've ever met." His blue eyes danced warm pleasure in her.

"Yeah. She's real smart," Hamish agreed.

The sound of a plane taking off distracted all three of

them. They looked up, no one saying anything until the Westlake Cessna had zoomed overhead and disappeared beyond the line of trees.

Hamish spoke first. "She's gone," he said in a tone of wonder, then turned questioning eyes to his father. "Did you tell her to go, Dad?"

He frowned. "You never tell a neighbour to go, Hamish. You always extend hospitality to accommodate them as far as you can."

"Yeah, I know." He kicked at the stones underfoot. "It's just that she usually stays."

"I guess she decided not to this time."

Taylor's gaze turned to Angie, piercingly blue, sweeping for any concern provoked by Diane Westlake's visit, determined on wiping it out. Angie stared back at him, her insides quivering with joy. There was no double game being played. This man stood with her.

"Was it 'cause you came out here for Angie?"

Hamish's question jolted them out of their intense absorption in each other. Both of them had momentarily forgotten his presence. Angie's nerves leapt with alarm at the thought they had given themselves away, that the boy had seen or sensed what was happening between them. Certainly there was a speculative look on his face.

"Diane could have many reasons for going home, Hamish," Taylor answered equably. "It's our job to look after our own people. I put that responsibility first. I'm sure Diane understood why I came out here."

"For Angie," Hamish repeated pointedly.

"Yes," his father agreed.

Hamish looked smugly satisfied. He glanced at Angie, his eyes dancing with mischief. "Maybe *you* knocked out the teeth, Angie." He chomped his jaw up and down in mock gobbling, then laughed as though all the cares of his world had been lifted from his shoulders.

Taylor was bemused. "What's this about?"

"Private joke," Angie said, smiling in relief. She'd proved to be a spoke in Diane's wheel! Hamish didn't mind if his father liked his governess, so long as the crocodile was de-toothed.

"Yeah. Private joke, Dad," he gleefully echoed. "Good thing I asked Angie to come riding with me."

Taylor smiled. "It was a good thought, Hamish, but we should be heading home now."

"Okay. I tethered our horses to the old swing tree."

He set off, his head high, a lively spring in his step, no kicking at stones.

Angie started to follow.

Taylor caught her hand, wrapping it in his warmth and sending an electric charge up her arm with an intimate little squeeze from his long, sensual fingers. His eyes were lightly quizzical. "Am I to be let in on the secret?"

She shrugged. "It should hardly be a secret to you that Diane Westlake is not one of Hamish's favourite people."

He sighed, rolling his eyes in an appeal for understanding. "Neither were you until today. Now, suddenly, you're in his good books. Want to tell me why?"

"I seem to be improving upon acquaintance."

He chuckled, pleased it was so. "I was worried he might do some mischief, without meaning you any harm."

"I think we're past that. He was aware I was trusting him and he honoured the trust."

"Glad to hear it."

Taylor did not relinquish her hand as they trailed after Hamish. It made Angie feel secure enough to say,

"Hamish was upset because Jessie repeated some gossip about you and Diane, suggesting a marriage between you was on the cards."

He heaved an exasperated sigh. "That's Thelma's fond notion. I told her last night it wasn't on. Diane is Adam Westlake's daughter and I extend the courtesy due to her. No more, no less, Angie."

Last night!

And Diane turned up today.

Taylor might be blind to the ramifications of that co-incidence but Angie certainly wasn't. Diane may well have played out a "sweetness and light" role with him, holding back her real interest while she surveyed the situation. Once Taylor had shown his caring for the governess, the lady had flown off, retaining her cover of the valued neighbour's daughter. Angie knew she, herself, would sound like a jealous bitch if she gave her reading of the other woman.

Diane must be in a fury of frustration, Angie thought, but she was clever enough to take herself out of any danger of showing it. A crocodile...waiting on the bank...watching for her best chance to pounce...and determined not to blow it prematurely.

Taylor had probably dismissed his wife's description as neurotic. God only knew what sly manipulation Diane Westlake had used to damage his marriage further, but Angie had no difficulty in imagining her stirring the pot behind Taylor's back. The resolution needed was not to fall prey to it herself.

Taylor had come to her.

He cared about her.

She had to hang on to that and not let any outside influence affect her belief in it.

Hamish was holding the horses ready to go. Taylor

helped Angie mount hers, his hands spanning her waist, lingering there until he was sure she was steady in the saddle. "I'm truly okay at this, but thanks," she said.

He grinned. "My pleasure."

And she knew he wanted any excuse to touch her.

Hamish's good humour was not at all dimmed by these familiarities. He looked upon Angie with a benevolent glow, his elation at Diane's departure still very much in play. They rode back to the homestead at a leisurely pace, the three of them abreast, Angie in the middle, being looked after by the two Maguires.

Conversation about the work of the day flowed naturally between father and son, though Angie wasn't excluded from it. For the most part she was content to remain quiet, listening to the nuances of their life pattern here, noting their mutual affinity with the land, the importance they placed on maintenance for the successful running of the station, and seeing how much Hamish wanted to be like his father, adopting his attitudes as though they seeped into him, like a process of osmosis.

The two of them were a unit, belonging together as she never had to either of her parents or her aunt. Again she felt the emptiness of floating outside a charmed circle, able to see it, touch it, even taste it. But that wasn't enough. It would never be enough. She yearned to be inside. Especially with this man.

She looked at him, unaware of the naked need in her eyes. He caught her glance. Instantly a blaze of desire ignited, as though it had been simmering below his surface composure all along, waiting only for a spark from her to burst into flame. Angie wrenched her gaze away, feeling the flare of heat racing to her face as her heart pumped faster. She was suddenly conscious of her breasts swelling with excitement, her legs spread apart

over the rhythmic movement of the horse, her thighs
rubbing against the saddle, her bottom slightly bouncing.

Erotic images blasted any sane thoughts from her
mind. Earthy, animal smells assailed her nostrils. She
peeked at Taylor's hands, loosely holding the reins;
strong, controlling hands, knowing how to touch, how
to mould, how to lead her into the mating act with both
tenderness and exhilarating power. Her gaze slid to his
hard, muscular thighs, so aggressively male, bringing the
more intimate part of his manhood vividly to mind.

"I'll look after the horses, Hamish," Taylor said as
they approached the gate to the stockyard beside the
barn. "You'd best take your saddle into the tack room
then race up to the house and wash for dinner. Thelma
won't be pleased if you're late."

He wanted time alone with her!

"Angie might need help with her saddle," Hamish
commented.

"Thanks, but I really should do it myself. Joe has
taught me how, and I want to practise it," she quickly
answered, allying herself with Taylor in pressing the boy
to leave them.

"Okay." Hamish grinned at her. "You've done really
well, Angie. Haven't even looked like falling off."

She smiled back. "You were very patient with me. It
made me feel safe."

"As Dad says, it's our job to look after our own people," he proudly declared.

Our own people.

Angie wished that meant more than employees.

The trick was going to be not to disgrace herself when
dismounting. There was a weakness coursing through
her legs from thinking of what Taylor intended, what

she wanted him to do, need and desire brewing an inner meltdown she could barely contain.

Somehow she managed to get her feet safely onto the ground. The next few minutes were virtually a blur. Hamish rushing around, Taylor lifting his own saddle onto the stockyard railing, then helping with hers, opening the gate, yarding the horses.

"See you later, Dad, Angie," Hamish called, taking off on his run to the house.

They waved. Taylor closed the gate, picked up his saddle again, and walked beside Angie to the barn. Without a word, they entered the dimly lit cavernous building and moved to the partitioned section where the riding tack was stored, bridles on hooks, saddles on trestles. The feelings they shared seemed too powerful for speech, as though talk could only be absurdly superficial, detracting from the momentum of reaching safe privacy where expression could take the course they both craved.

As soon as they had unburdened themselves of the riding gear, Taylor swung her toward him. Angie's arms locked around his neck as he swept her body hard against his. Their mouths collided, great breakers of hunger rolling through their kiss, drawing and sucking and crashing with passionate force, a wild urgent plunder that drove them into feverish need.

He backed against the wall, dragging her in between his thighs, kneading her buttocks, pushing them inward, thrusting her closer, moulding her to the rampant hardness of his arousal. She felt as though she was shattering inside, desperate for his strength to hold her together. He plucked her shirt out of her jeans and a hand snaked up the curve of her spine to unclip her bra. The clawing of his fingers shot shivers of sensation over her skin.

His mouth broke from hers. "Angie..." A heated

groan. He spun her around, her back to him. "...I have to touch." His fingers dislodging her loosened bra, sweeping the naked fullness of her breasts, diving down to the waist stud of her jeans, pulling it apart, his other hand on the zipper, then inside her panties, pushing through the soft bush of hair to the intimate fold below, stroking her into hot liquid.

She swayed against him, her head falling back on his shoulder, and his mouth fastened on her neck, the hunger even more raw and needful, his hand roving greedily over her breasts while other fingers were delving into her, her body clenching around them, convulsing, wanting, wanting, wanting...the thick roll of him against her buttocks, muffled by clothes, and her voice crying out, wild and strange as she had not heard it before, "Let me feel you, too..."

She didn't have the strength to do it herself. She was quivering from the bombardment of sensation, and everything within her seemed to be hanging on a pinnacle of anticipation that only the feel of him could satisfy. His arm hooked around her waist, supporting her as he undid his jeans, then pushed hers down, and at last there was the slide of his hard flesh against hers, the delight of its power travelling between her legs, stroking her with its heat, wonderful slippery pleasure, exquisitely tantalising, not enough.

"Please..."

"Angie, I can't." Despair cracking through his voice. "The risk... I wasn't expecting this."

"It's safe... I swear..." Frantic, aching. "...You must..."

She bent forward, leaning on one of the saddles slung over the trestle, reaching through the apex of her thighs for him, pressing, needing, and with a desperate, animal cry he drove into her, filling her, possessing her in urgent, shocking haste, yet her body revelled in it, loved it, exulted in its ability to take and give as the same awesome thrust came again and again, feeling fiercer, hotter, larger, longer, rocking her with ecstatic waves of ever-increasing intensity.

His arms were hugging her, his hands clutching her breasts, his body mounted over hers. She had the erotic image of them riding together, the smell of leather around them, and it was his world they were climbing and she belonged to it with him, indivisibly together, and he was saying her name over and over and everything was pounding until they burst over the peak, climaxing with a sweet violence that flowed and flooded and warmed and soothed. And at the end of it, the hoarse, emotion-laden whisper of, "Angie..."

Through the swimming mush of her mind drifted a wondrous, beautiful, heart-hugging thought. This territory was hers, not Diane Westlake's. Taylor was holding her locked to him, his mouth pressing kisses on her skin, breathing *her* name, and there was no room at all for a crocodile to pounce.

CHAPTER THIRTEEN

FOR many weeks the men had been mustering from camp to camp, branding, culling, driving the stock in, and today was the big day. The road train had come this morning and loading the selected herd onto it was underway. From here cattle would be taken to Darwin, then shipped to Indonesia. The logistics of organising it all certainly demonstrated how big a business running a station like Giralang was.

Angie had declared time off from school for the duration and she and the three children hung on the stockyard railings, watching what to her was an amazing scene.

Taylor stood high on the fence by the gate, overseeing the drive onto the loading ramp. He was using a two-way radio to keep in constant communication with Joe Cameron, the head stockman. Leo sat on a specially fitted high chair above the last yard, keeping book on each loading.

The cattle were big red Brahman crosses, and their hooves kicked up clouds of red dust as they were relentlessly moved through the yards by the men on their horses, keeping the herd going with electric prodders and plastic tubes, the cattle dogs circling watchfully, ready to round up any straying beast. The occasional breakaway brought heart-kicking excitement, but both men and dogs were incredibly skilful at maintaining control.

The bellowing from the cattle, shouting and swearing from the men, barking from the dogs, all the jostling and

tramping provided continual movement and noise on a
scale that bombarded every sense, stamping an indelible
reality of what this outback life encompassed; its danger,
its vitality, its challenge, the sweat and the heat and the
dust, the sheer bigness of it all, dwarfing anything Angie
had known before.

It made a city existence feel unreal, as though people
only played with toys there, surrounding themselves
with manufactured objects, having lost touch with basic
nature. Values were placed on things that were meaningless to people bred to this land. It was suddenly very
clear to Angie why they held such a reserve about city
people. The gap was so great. She understood it now.
She could see it, feel it, and she knew she would never
feel quite right in a city again.

There was something about all this that went soul-
deep. She had heard the outback spoken of as a vast
emptiness, but there was substance here, solid substance
that emitted a sense of constancy. It wouldn't change
overnight. It couldn't be taken away. It represented life
in its most primal state and it remained true to its nature.
Somehow these qualities soothed the uncertainties that
had plagued Angie most of her life. She didn't feel displaced. Being here felt good. Right.

In the four months she'd been at Giralang, she
couldn't recall ever being bored. There was so much to
learn, all of it of interest to her. Taylor, of course, was
so inextricably bound up in the place, it was impossible
to separate him from it, which, Angie realised, had its
influence on her. All the same, she truly did feel she
could live out the rest of her life here...with him.

The tantalising question was...would he want her to?

Today he looked very much the cattle king he was,
standing tall above the melee, dominating it with his

authority. Yet he wasn't an arrogant dictator driven by a sense of power or ego, simply a man who saw what had to be done and did it, who shouldered responsibility and didn't shirk from doing anything he expected of his men, which earned both their liking and respect. They all said Giralang was a good station to work on.

Angie knew why. It was the quality of leadership Taylor gave them; caring, fair and firm. In her teaching experience, it was always the principal who set the tone of the school, making a remarkable difference to how well it operated. So much depended upon the man in control. The men instinctively trusted Taylor.

She had, too, the night he'd rescued her from Brian. She'd entrusted him with much more of herself since then and not been disappointed anywhere along the line. He had learnt to trust her, too, even putting the contraception issue aside once she assured him she was on the pill. Yet she did not really know what he felt for her, beyond the physical intimacy they shared. She suspected the failure of his marriage still haunted him. He seemed content to be sexually satisfied, living each day as it came with her, not looking any further.

"I'm starving," Wayne declared with feeling. "Must be lunchtime. Let's go get something to eat."

He was off the railings before Jessie began to scramble down after him. "Wayne, we don't have to go up to the homestead kitchen," she called in the big-sisterly, bossy tone she tended to use with the boys. "Our mums are helping the men's cook today. They're getting stuff ready for the barbecue tonight."

His face lit up. "Yeah. We could pinch some of that."

"I didn't mean..." Jessie huffed in annoyance. Wayne had already taken to his heels and she ran to catch up with him.

Hamish hadn't budged. He grinned at Angie. "Wayne will get a cuff around his ears from Bill if he's not careful."

The men's cook didn't take kindly to a disorderly taking of the food he prepared. He used to be in the army and he kept strict account of everything. Angie grinned back. "Serve him right. I think we'd better keep out of Bill's way and go up to the house for our lunch. Or would you rather stay here and I'll bring some sandwiches back for you?"

"No. I could do with a long drink. Get the dust out of my mouth."

"Me, too."

Taylor's head turned sharply toward them as they climbed down from their perch on the railings, his gaze catching Angie's with an alertness that made her realise he'd been aware of her presence all along, despite his concentration on the work in hand.

"Lunch!" she yelled, pointing up to the house.

He nodded and waved them on, quickly returning his attention to where it was needed. Just one glance, reaffirming the close connection between them, and it put a happy spring into her step. She smiled at Hamish, glad he didn't seem to mind the obvious friendship she had with Taylor.

"I suppose someone will feed your father and the men sometime."

"Bill sends out lunch-packs. They all eat on the go today, then have a huge feed up tonight at the barbecue." His eyes sparkled with anticipation. "It's always a great night, Angie."

"It's a great day."

He laughed then cocked a measuring look at her. "You really like it here, don't you?"

"Yes."

"Is it 'cause of Dad?"

"He's part of it," she answered honestly. "I think your father's a great man."

"He looks happy with you," came the speculative observation, then the rueful comment, "He wasn't happy with my mum."

Angie took a deep breath, acutely aware of sensitive ground. "I'm sorry it was like that, Hamish," she said quietly.

"It was 'cause she wasn't happy here," he returned matter-of-factly.

"I guess it strikes people differently."

"Yeah. Dad said you were different. And you are. I'm glad you came to Giralang, Angie. It's been real good."

"It's been good for me, too."

"Are you going to stay?"

"As long as your father will let me."

He nodded with an air of satisfaction. "I reckon Dad will keep you. When he's happy with someone he always tries to keep them on Giralang. It makes everything work better."

A very simple equation in Hamish's mind, but not quite so simple in Angie's. Nevertheless, the boy's acceptance of her as a good part of their lives was heart-warming. His linking her with his mother carried less certain connotations. Did he sense how intimate she was with Taylor, or was he harking back to his initial hostility toward her? Whatever he was thinking, at least he displayed a far more positive attitude toward her than he had to Diane Westlake.

Whom they hadn't seen since her aborted visit two months ago.

But who would be very much in evidence at the picnic races, only three weeks away now.

Angie suspected Diane was bound to make the festive weekend uncomfortable for her, one way or another, but there was no point in worrying about it. Besides, as long as Taylor supported her, surely other people would respect her position with him.

Thelma was concocting a giant trifle in a huge plastic bowl when Angie and Hamish entered the kitchen after having washed off the dust from their faces and hands in the laundry. They helped themselves to food and drink while Hamish chatted on to his aunt about the cattle drive.

Thelma rarely directed conversation at Angie. She wasn't exactly rude but Angie was well aware the older woman hadn't thawed in her attitude toward her. If anything, it was more frosty. The *city woman* tag had probably been updated to *loose city woman* since she and Taylor had become lovers.

"Come on, Angie. Let's get back," Hamish said eagerly, refuelled for the afternoon. He grinned at his aunt. "She doesn't want to miss anything."

"I daresay it is a novelty for her," came the sardonic comment, her grey eyes flicking a derisive dismissal of any lasting interest by Angie in station business.

Her policy of non-confrontation with Taylor's aunt suddenly wore very thin. Usually Angie let such comments slide past her, believing only time would show the older woman they had no sting or power. Somehow today was different. She wanted to correct the judgment Thelma kept making.

"You go ahead, Hamish," she said with an encouraging smile. "I have a couple of things to do before I leave the house."

"Okay," he agreed obligingly. "Don't be long though."

"I won't."

Angie waited until he was out of earshot, then quietly asked, "Why do you want to drive me away, Thelma? What harm am I doing?"

The older woman stopped sprinkling coconut over the trifle and eyed her with steely dislike. "You've got your honeyed claws into both Taylor and Hamish and it will rip them apart when you decide you've had enough."

"I don't think I'll ever have enough."

Thelma snorted. "Sex doesn't cover everything, however good it is."

"No, but it doesn't have to. I like what's here, Thelma."

Icy scepticism. "The novelty will wear off. As it did with Trish."

"She didn't love Taylor," Angie said with certainty.

A sneer of contempt. "You city people fall in and out of love so many times the divorce courts can't keep up with you."

"I'm not talking about a fleeting physical attraction, Thelma. I love Taylor for the man he is...honest and trustworthy and strong and dependable and caring. To me he's not a glamorous cattle king. He's a king amongst men, towering over everyone else in the qualities that mean most to me. And I know this land and the demands it makes on him is an integral part of what he is, and it answers what I've been seeking all my life."

For once, the older woman was stumped for a reply, arrested by the passionate conviction in Angie's words.

A sad irony twisted her mouth as Angie added, "It won't be me who cries 'enough,' Thelma. It will be Taylor. If he wants to."

Silence. Nothing but a blank stare from the older woman.

Angie turned away and left the kitchen, not knowing if anything she said had sunk home or met an impenetrable shield. Perhaps she had spoken out prematurely and only time could prove whatever Thelma needed proven. It was probably impossible for anyone else to look into her own heart and see the truth.

But she knew it. She had never known anything so clearly. And much, much later that day, after the cattle had all been loaded and the road train had departed, and everyone on the station had dispersed to their various habitats to clean up for the barbecue, Angie's deep hunger for the man she loved led her straight into his bathroom where the shower was spilling down at full power, full heat.

He didn't hear her enter. Through the steamed-up glass door she could see his back was turned to her, his head tilted to the streaming water, fingers raking shampoo suds from his hair. Angie had already showered but she couldn't wait for him to finish. She discarded her clothes, opened the shower door and stepped in with him, sliding her arms around his waist, pushing her fingers down over his flat stomach, tangling with him intimately, yearningly as she gently rubbed her body against his.

He went utterly still, as though he was holding his breath, focusing all of himself on the sensations she aroused. She felt the power of him surging under her touch, rising, hardening, becoming fully erect and she revelled in the feeling of owning him, if only this much. She kissed his back and murmured, ''I thought you were wonderful today, holding control over all that frazzling activity.''

His breath whooshed out and he turned, smiling. "Is this my reward?"

She smiled back through the water. "I've been watching you and wanting you for hours."

"Days, weeks, months, years," he said huskily, lifting her, holding her against him as she sank slowly, exultantly, down to meet and engulf the eager shaft of his manhood, easing onto it with exquisitely felt anticipation.

He pressed her back against the wall, bracing himself to start thrusting, but he kissed her first, a long drowning kiss that made her feel both languid and frantic, loving it but desperate for more of him, hungry for all he could give her. She flexed and pushed at him, driving for the motion she wanted, needed, and he responded wildly, rearing back and plunging forward, lifting her and letting her fall to a pounding rhythm, her body slithering against the wall, water cascading around them, the steam of heat and flesh a hot erotic mist, his hands kneading her buttocks, and inside her, the sweet building of peaks of pleasure, higher, sharper, and the yielding depths within grasping for the utmost pinnacle, and there it was, a glorious, triumphant fusion of giving to each other, possessing each other, sharing and belonging.

"You're the one who's wonderful, Angie," he whispered, kissing her in a rain of fervour.

And as she slowly floated down from heaven, she touched his face and said, "I hope you always think that, Taylor."

"How could I not?" he answered, his eyes so intense they seemed to tunnel into her soul. "You're the best thing that ever happened to me, Angie."

Then love me, she silently begged. *Love me and never let me go.*

But he eased her onto her feet and washed away the aftermath of their lovemaking, tenderly, thoroughly, then dried them both, and while still together, they were apart again, without the words Angie desperately wanted to hear being spoken.

The hunger in her heart throbbed on.

CHAPTER FOURTEEN

THE barbecue was in full swing; hearty appetites being satisfied, everyone in a relaxed, happy mood, joking, laughing, pleased that the work of the day had been achieved without any mishap and all set to party until exhaustion set in. Taylor enjoyed the lively camaraderie of such nights as this…the whole Giralang family celebrating together, their teamwork and unity of purpose understood and appreciated as an integral part of their lives. As natural as breathing.

Did Angie comprehend how deep it went?

Was she herself affected by it, or did her interest have more the collective delight of a keen observer being subjected to a new experience?

Taylor wished he knew. They'd been sharing their meal with Joe and Sue Cameron, the head stockman and his wife having become firm friends with Angie. Taylor watched the lovely vivacity of her face as she chatted to Sue, sharing her impressions of the day. There was no doubt she'd been caught up in the excitement of it, and awed by the skills involved in loading the herd onto the road train.

Something about it had moved her to come to him in the shower. He wasn't sure what. Only that it had been urgent and strongly primitive, as much of the sex between them was, but he'd always felt that came mainly from him with Angie being carried along with it. Yet this time…strange the feeling it had given him, being locked in her embrace while she took possession of him.

The sense of wanting from her had been so strong, and though intensely exciting for him, he wasn't sure he'd answered it for her.

She gave him such incredible pleasure, the *whys* for it had hardly seemed to matter. It happened and he was grateful she'd come into his life. She offered—gave— all the good feelings he'd ever imagined possible between a man and woman, companionably as well as sexually. Now, suddenly, the *whys* had taken on more importance. He wanted to keep Angie with him.

"Hey, Angie!" It was Chris Roland, one of the young jackeroos strolling past to get second helpings at the barbecue. He gave her a wide grin. "You got a taste of cattle dust today."

She laughed. "I sure did."

"We got every one of 'em in without injury," he crowed.

"I thought all you men were incredibly brave and clever," she said, glowing with admiration.

"Just doin' our job," Chris manfully downplayed, but Taylor noticed every lad amongst them looked smugly pleased with themselves and took on an extra swagger as they moved on.

"We'll make an outback woman of you yet, Angie," Joe teased, having already chalked up the credit of making a horsewoman of her.

"That, Joe, would be my proudest moment," she answered, and the golden shine of her amber eyes moved directly to Taylor.

His heart kicked. Did she mean it? Or did she simply have the knack of saying the right thing at the right time to make people feel good?

She'd only been here four months. It wasn't long

enough to make a clear-cut judgment on such a vast lifestyle change. Was it?

He tried to quell the wild hope running through his veins. All this was new to her, new and different, safely distant from the unhappy associations Slater must have left her with.

But she *was* happy here. He couldn't be mistaken about that. Happy with him and everyone else, except Thelma who remained stiff-necked with prejudice, though less than usual tonight. The party seemed to have loosened her up a bit.

The children, especially Hamish, had blossomed with new confidence. As a governess, Angie was unquestionably the best he could have employed. And true to her own word, she wasn't a flirt or a tease. There wasn't a man on the station who didn't like and respect her. The women, too.

She had a very appealing common touch that generated friendly responses, whereas Trish…well, Trish had tended to put everyone's backs up with her air of condescension and expecting special respect as the boss's wife—respect she'd never earned as a person in her own right.

But then Trish had never tried to fit in here, never cared enough to try, not for herself, nor for him, nor their son, and the initial pleasure of queening it over everyone had proved empty all too soon. Angie *did* fit in, though whether this was the instinctive reaction of a chameleon who'd been hurt in too many moves and was intent on avoiding all trouble, or a natural response to the life here, Taylor wasn't sure.

"Angie…" Hamish ran up, urgently eager. "Come on, quick. Bill's uncovering the second earth oven with more potatoes and stuff. You missed the first one."

She leapt up from the bench seat. "Right! Excuse me, people. Got to go and see this."

Hamish grabbed her hand and they were off together, their mutual pleasure in the show-and-tell exercise evident. Taylor grinned after them. It was great to see his son being a natural boy again and he deeply appreciated the way Angie promoted it in him.

Sue stood up, collecting their plates. "Anyone for seconds?"

"Might have another baked potato, love," Joe answered. "With the trimmings."

"What about you, Taylor?"

He shook his head. "I'll hold on for sweets, thanks, Sue."

She left them, giving Joe a speaking look before she turned away. Taylor wondered what message she was transmitting to her husband. Joe cleared his throat, an ominous sign. It invariably heralded touchy business. Taylor cocked his eyebrow, inviting his head stockman's confidence. As usual, Joe was not about to be hurried into coming to the point.

"Reckon you've got a good thing going with Angie, Taylor," he started.

"That I have, Joe," he agreed warmly.

"The men think she's a bit of all right. They'd do anything for her, you know."

"I'm glad they feel that."

Joe nodded a few times. "Kids are happy with her."

"Yes, they are."

"So are the women. Even though Angie's city bred, they reckon she's got her heart in the right place."

Taylor nodded. He didn't need to be told Angie had a good heart. She was more than fair in her dealings, caring, giving, and very perceptive and considerate of others' feelings. She never asked too much of anyone, was always ready to oblige reasonable requests, and seemed content within herself. All in all, she was a very special person, to him a unique woman he would hate to lose.

Not just because of the sex. *She* made that wonderful...the person she was inside, the woman who complemented the man in him. Perhaps his instincts had somehow picked that up from their very first meeting at the Brisbane Hilton. The feelings she aroused then had been coloured by his own physical frustrations, but she'd been touching him in other ways long before he'd taken her to bed with him...her intelligence, her honesty, her enterprise, her courage.

The attraction was long past skin-deep. He suspected it always had been, though he hadn't allowed himself to dwell on it, upholding a barrier of caution against the uncertainty of a future with her. He wished he could set the uncertainty aside.

Proud to be an outback woman...fact or fantasy?

Maybe Angie had a need to fit in. A desperate need. Her pleas at the interview had held a desperate edge. He'd thought he understood it when he found out about Slater, but there could have been other underlying factors driving her, as well, a seeking for something that had always eluded her, perhaps a sense of identity she'd never found.

Was there an overwhelming need to belong to someone or somewhere? A person and place she could call her own? Any person, any place, as long as they gave her a sense of belonging?

He kept coming back to the electric moment in the shower when she'd claimed possession of him, and then her desperate desire for his possession.

Was *he* the man Angie wanted…or did he *represent* something she wanted?

Did it matter…as long as she stayed with him?

"Picnic races coming up soon," Joe said, cutting into Taylor's private reverie.

"Mmm…a good break for the men."

"Yeah. There's a couple of horses they want to enter. Reckon they'd have a chance of winning."

"Arrange it then, Joe."

"Will do. No worries. 'Cept Angie."

Taylor frowned. "What's Angie got to do with it?"

Joe eyed him directly. "Angie will be coming with us, won't she?"

"Of course."

"Well, you know how women talk," Joe said meaningly.

Gossip was a fact of life. The thought of Angie being wounded by it twisted his gut. "What are you getting at, Joe?" he asked sharply, determined on straightening out the situation in no uncertain terms.

Joe's grimace held apologetic appeal. "Just don't like the idea of Angie getting hurt. Sue reckons Diane Westlake will be gunning for her. Diane…she can come over as sweet as pie but Sue says she's damned good at sticking the knife in and giving it a sly twist. Thought you should know so you can watch out."

Diane! The singular accusation of bitchy malice jolted him. It instantly raised a string of uncomfortable memories. "Trish used to say that but I never saw it myself," he commented, troubled that he should have given more weight to Trish's venomous reaction to Diane instead of dismissing it as neurotic nonsense. Joe's wife was one of the most down-to-earth women Taylor knew. He couldn't dismiss her opinion lightly.

"Sue says men can be right blind about such things," Joe followed up, nodding his head, accepting his wife's words as undoubted truth. "Wouldn't be good if Diane made Angie feel bad, Taylor."

Behind his back! That's what Trish had always claimed. It had seemed so alien to the face Diane presented to him, still did, but he wasn't about to risk being wrong about it. Especially since she had shown interest in him since Trish had died. If Diane thought Angie was spiking her chances at the marriage Thelma was in favour of…and that raised questions about Diane's last visit…like what had gone on behind his back then?

Hamish had taken Angie out riding…the sudden sympathy between them…nothing said to him, but Diane flying off before she had to face him and Angie together. Sly…he didn't like it. He didn't like it one bit. His relationship with Angie meant too much to let Diane sour it in any way.

"I appreciate the advice, Joe."

"Hope I'm not speaking out of turn."

"Not at all. A timely warning never goes astray. Give my thanks to Sue."

The two women were on their way back. Taylor felt a surge of turbulent emotion as he watched Angie coming toward him, so warmly beautiful and infinitely desirable, yet what stirred him most was the memory of how vulnerable she had looked the night he'd rescued her from Slater. He didn't want anyone to hurt her. Ever again. And by God, he'd protect her with all that he was!

CHAPTER FIFTEEN

ANGIE couldn't help feeling a little apprehensive over what kind of welcome she would receive at the picnic races, being a newcomer, a governess from the city who didn't know the ropes, and commonly known to be connected to Taylor Maguire in more than an employee sense. She didn't doubt she would have the ready support of everyone from Giralang, with the possible exception of Thelma, but Diane Westlake could prove a snake in the grass, if not a crocodile.

Within hours of arriving at the Westlake Station, her fears appeared to be groundless. Diane was all charm and warm hospitality in her greeting, more than backed up by her father who was brimming with good humour and clearly on very friendly terms with Taylor, welcoming him with a huge grin and a vigorous handshake. He was a big barrel-chested man with a voice to match.

"I hear your men have brought a couple of promising nags," he boomed.

"Could give yours a run for their money," Taylor replied, his eyes twinkling.

Adam laughed and ran an appreciative eye over Angie, winking at her as he said, "Taylor's a dark horse but he sure knows how to pick a fine filly." It was a compliment, plain and simple, no hint of anything but admiration in his eyes.

"Angie Cordell, Adam," Taylor introduced.

"A pleasure to meet you, Angie." A warm handclasp. "Diane tells me you're from the city. There'll be other city folk coming in for the weekend. Hope they won't make you homesick.''

''Not a chance,'' Angie assured him, and everyone else within earshot. ''I love being here.''

''No place like it,'' he said proudly. He looked askance at his daughter. ''Though I don't suppose your hotshot financier will agree.''

''You never know, Dad,'' Diane said archly, her eyes flashing some indefinable challenge at Angie. Somehow it seemed both sly and smug, as though she nursed a secret which both amused her and made her feel superior.

Adam rolled his eyes in mock chagrin. ''She's got herself a city boyfriend. Diane, who was born in the saddle. Can you make sense of that for me, Taylor?''

Tit for tat? Angie wondered. Wanting to show Taylor he was a fool, trying to mix oil with water?

''Well, Adam, there could always be an outback man under the city clothes, trying to get out,'' Taylor answered dryly, curving an arm around Angie's shoulders, drawing her into sharing a smile with him. ''I've had my prejudice beaten into the dust by the way Angie's taken to the life. She's a constant marvel to me.''

Her heart turned over. His vivid blue eyes were warm and loving, no doubts at all. Diane and her city boyfriend were nothing to him. Totally irrelevant. And in an instant, the worry Diane had stirred disappeared and a surge of happiness lifted her spirits. It didn't matter what anyone else thought as long as Taylor wanted her at his side.

So it continued that first afternoon with everyone they met, Taylor holding her close, smoothly performing introductions, subtly impressing the fact she was his woman and very much part of the life at Giralang, not someone to be condescended to as a temporary figure from the city. It was like being handed a golden passport to acceptance, removing all grounds for discord or reservation. Each meeting turned into a happy exchange of news, everyone taking it for granted she understood what they were talking about. She was one of them.

The legendary outback hospitality was here in abundance, no frills or pretensions, a carefree friendly open warmth that soaked into Angie and spread a wonderfully festive atmosphere. Fifteen cattle stations had set up elaborate camps along the river bank, tents for sleeping quarters, marquees to house the eating tables and enough supplies of food and drink to satisfy the fierce appetites forged over a week of competitive fun.

In a way it was like Christmas in the middle of the year. Power generators attached to each camp ran deep freezers filled with enough turkey, steak and ham to feed an army, and at every marquee they were offered champagne, rum, whisky or beer. It was a time of reunion, of commiseration on bad luck, celebration of good fortune, and the general pleasure of congenial company with mutual interests. Angie was swept up in it all and loved every minute of it, loved even more the sense of belonging Taylor gave her.

Many people had arrived up to ten days beforehand, including most of the men from Giralang, bringing their horses and supervising their training for the races, trucking in the equipment and setting up camp, getting everything ready for the big week. A three-deep tier of tents were lined up with military precision, a procession of billowing canvas and guy ropes stretching from either side of the main hospitality marquee which was run by the Westlake Station and centred to face the arena where the main festival activity took place.

It wasn't all horse-racing. Most of the fun was centred around the children. A schoolroom was set up by itinerant teachers who gave the school of the air children a taste of lessons in a real classroom situation, plus the opportunity of learning how to mix and play with those whom they only knew from their voices on the radio. Angie was involved in this, along with the other governesses and mothers who supervised their children at home.

Best of all though were the games organised for the children. They played a loose form of cricket, touch football, tug-of-war, tunnel ball—all team games that frequently involved their parents and a great deal of barracking and excitement. They laughed themselves silly over novelty events like the father and son three-legged race. When mothers were required as partners, Hamish insisted Angie stand in with him, and Taylor stood on the sidelines cheering them on.

Angie couldn't remember ever having such a happy time. She was occasionally aware of Diane swanning around in the background, playing gracious hostess, but nothing the other woman said or did intruded on Angie's sense of well-being. The days rolled by, gathering a momentum toward the big races at the weekend, one of Giralang's horses emerging as a favourite to take out the main event, stirring great pride and joy amongst the men.

Angie saw the plane fly in on Friday morning and thought it was probably bringing the city visitors, but she didn't really relate them to herself. She'd moved a long way from having anything in common with them. Diane was welcome to her new boyfriend. Angie even wished her joy of him.

The schoolroom packed up that morning, the teachers having established a wonderful camaraderie amongst the children which would undoubtedly boost their enjoyment in the answer sessions on school of the air, the familiarity from this week still fresh in their minds so they could easily fit faces to voices. For Angie, meeting the mothers and other governesses had wiped out her reluctance to join in the radio chat sessions. She eagerly looked forward to keeping their acquaintance going.

The stroll back to the Giralang camp for lunch was interrupted several times by new friends calling out to her and Hamish. As they passed the Westlake marquee, a hail from Diane caused no stab of unease. The unfailing support by both Taylor and Hamish had given Angie a confidence and security the other woman couldn't shake. She turned, a smile of inquiry flashing forth.

It froze on her face.

The crocodile was back. Two crocodiles, their teeth bared in readiness to mash Angie in their jaws. It was the second one who caused her heart to cramp and shot icicles down her spine... Diane's city boyfriend...the hotshot financier...none other than Brian Slater!

She felt the blood draining from her face, had the sickening sensation of the ground shifting under her feet. No place was safe anymore. The oppression she thought she had escaped pressed in on her again...the lies, the twisted thinking, the refusal to accept rejection, the sheer perverseness of his pursuit of her, the frightening persistence insidiously eating away at her freedom, trapping her in a web of devious plays that reduced her to a quivering mess of vulnerability.

Brian...Diane...two of a kind, she realised, pursuing their quarry with self-centred relentlessness, but the insight did no good. She stood like a mesmerised rabbit as they bore down on her, disbelief mixing with horror at the sheer malice of what couldn't be a coincidence.

The knowingness in Diane's eyes...her smug pleasure in it...the glitter of triumph in Brian's...his satisfaction in it...somehow they'd got together and planned this meeting, each for their own ends. Angie knew it in her gut, which was twisting into nauseous knots.

"Angie?" Hamish, sensing something wrong, stepped back to take her hand and stand with her.

It was no comfort. No protection, either. She couldn't even bring herself to glance at him. She couldn't tear her eyes off the approach of the two crocodiles, feeling the menace in every step they took toward her, struggling to raise a mental shield against the coming attack, to suppress the fear of the damage they wanted to wreak.

"Brian tells me you know each other," Diane opened up, her voice dripping with mock innocence.

"Angie..." Brian spread his arms as though he expected her to fall into them. "...Who'd have thought you'd be hiding out here?" His eyes exulted in having found her.

"Angie's not hiding," Hamish growled like a guard dog whose instincts were obviously registering something dangerous and hostile.

Brian laughed, his easy charm drawn into instant play. "I only meant she left Brisbane so abruptly we didn't have time to say goodbye..." He lifted his indulgent smile from Hamish to her. "...Did we, darling?"

It goaded her to answer, "I said goodbye, Brian. More than once. You chose not to listen."

"Well, we all make choices we regret," he returned smoothly.

"I don't regret mine," she bit out, clenching her teeth against his oily suggestiveness.

Diane came in with a smarmy warning. "Early days

yet, Angie. I always think it's rather short-sighted to
burn bridges.''

''What opinion do you have on someone who keeps
trying to build a bridge to nowhere?'' Angie flashed at
her, anger flooding over the fear.

Diane shrugged, her eyes derisively belittling Angie's
point as she answered, ''I guess it's all in one's sense
of vision. I have a long view of things myself.''

Angie suddenly had no doubt Trish had suffered from
Diane's *long view.*

''Besides, life is full of surprises,'' Brian said with
another megawatt smile.

Orchestrated by him, Angie thought bitterly.

''I know I'm going to be vastly entertained by this
outback weekend,'' he went on. ''Especially with you
here, Angie.''

''Angie's with me and Dad,'' Hamish piped up bel-
ligerently.

''Oh, Hamish!'' Diane laughed dismissively. ''A governess isn't on duty all the time. School's over now and
she's free to do as she wants.''

''Angie likes being with us,'' he retorted stubbornly.
''We're going to lunch now.'' He tugged at her hand.

The reinforced link with Taylor's son pulled Angie
out of the futile compulsion to face the obsessive drive
of these two destructive people. Argument won nothing
from them. Common sense would never prevail. No
stand would alter anything. There was only one course
to take, the one Brian had driven her to before. Walk
away.

''Yes, Hamish. We'll go now,'' she said, the bleak-
ness in her heart making the resolution sound too much
like defeat. Which it was, in a way. She simply couldn't
beat these people. She had no weapons to use against

them. Retreat…escape…but there was no safe place. Not even Giralang. Brian knew now. And he wouldn't let go. Neither would Diane.

"By the way," Diane slid in quickly, her eyes brightly challenging. "Dad wants you and Taylor to join us for lunch, Angie. You will pass on the invitation, won't you?"

"I'm looking forward to having your company," Brian said with relish.

"Dad is expecting you," Diane pressed, closing the trap with equal relish.

Taylor. Her heart ached with need as she walked away with his son. Taylor had saved her once. Maybe he could again.

CHAPTER SIXTEEN

ONE look at Hamish and Angie as they entered the marquee told Taylor something was badly wrong. His conversation with his aunt came to an abrupt halt as alarm kicked through his heart. Angie's face was pale and lifeless, her usual vivacity totally wiped out, all positive energy drained from her body. Hamish was virtually pulling her with him and his expression was fighting mad.

"Diane's got a man with her who upset Angie. And she was mean, too, underneath her crocodile smile," he declared heatedly, defying any correction to his judgment of the situation. "I don't care if she is our neighbour, she's real slimy, Dad. And so's he."

"The city boyfriend?" Taylor asked sharply of Angie, wanting to break through her air of bleak withdrawal.

She looked at him, her beautiful amber eyes glazed with hopelessness and slowly filling with tears. "It's Brian. Brian Slater," she choked out. "Diane brought him to me. She knew." Her head shook in helpless anguish. "She knew."

Even as his stunned mind groped to make sense of what she said, Taylor wrapped Angie in his arms and tried to soothe her distress with comforting caresses. Slater, the devious bastard, finding his way to Angie again. Through Diane, no doubt, but with her connivance? Surely not! "How could Diane have known about him? It must be coincidence, Angie."

160

"No," she sobbed. "I saw it in their eyes. The complicity. I can't think how...unless you told her."

The quiver of betrayal in her broken voice smote his heart. "No," he answered strongly. "I told Diane nothing about Slater. I swear it, Angie."

"About me, then." She lifted tear-washed eyes, searching for answers, however much they hurt. "The day she rode out to you at the leaking bore. You must have said something to lead her to Brian."

He shook his head, raking his memory, certain he'd kept Angie's private business absolutely private. "Not a word pertaining to your life before Giralang," he stated with conviction.

Her head sagged onto his shoulder. "It doesn't matter now," she said listlessly. "It's done. She wants to get rid of me. Somehow she found Brian and she's using him."

It was shock talking, he reasoned, the revival of trauma, the sense of persecution. It was neurotic to think...but hadn't he used that excuse to himself when Trish had ranted about Diane? Don't overlook anything, he cautioned himself. Angie had shown him many times she saw some things more clearly than he did. He had to believe her, protect her, take care she was never victimised again by anyone.

"Is he a bad man, Dad?" Hamish asked.

"Yes. Very bad. But don't worry, Hamish. I won't let him get near Angie again," Taylor vowed, determined on confronting the situation head-on.

"What about Diane?" Hamish's eyes burned with a steadfast belief in her badness, too, not the slightest doubt about Angie's accusation.

Faith and trust in him was obviously hanging in the balance and Taylor was instantly persuaded to give his son the assurance he wanted. "I'll deal with her, as well." Neither of them was about to ignore a source of pain to the woman who had given so much of herself to them.

"Go and fetch Gary and Joe and Bill," he commanded, a plan of action forming in his mind. "I want them on standby."

"Right!" his son replied with keen satisfaction, and raced off to do his part.

"I don't understand what's going on," Thelma pleaded, her face creased in concern and bewilderment at Angie's breakdown and what was ensuing from it. "What has this Brian Slater done?"

Angie shuddered. Taylor held her more tightly. "Angie got involved with him, not realising he was one of those possessive freaks who won't let go. He'd been stalking her for months before the job at Giralang came up. She needed it to get away from him."

"Oh! So that's why…" Her face drooped in pained regret and the gaze she turned on Angie was a confused mixture of guilt and sympathy. "You should have told me, Taylor. I said some harsh things. Made it difficult. Not welcome. Oh, dear!" She shook her head in self-chastisement. "I wasn't very friendly. If you'd only told me…"

"Angie wanted to leave it behind her, Thelma."

"Oh!" Her hands clapped her face in horror. "Oh, my God!" She stared at Taylor, completely stricken. "Maybe this dreadful situation is my fault. I didn't know it could lead to anything bad."

"What?" he snapped.

"Diane mustn't realise what kind of a man he is," she excused, clinging to her view of Adam's daughter.

"What part have you played in this, Thelma?" Taylor bored in.

She answered in a fluster. "It's just that…well, the day Diane came to Giralang, she wanted to know everything about Angie. I got out her résumé for the governess job from your filing cabinet and I left Diane with it while I…"

"So she had the information to track Angie's life in Brisbane," Taylor cut in, furious that her confidential papers had been misused.

"I didn't mean any harm," his aunt pleaded.

"Diane does, Thelma. She stuck barbs into Trish and she's trying to do the same to Angie. You'd better take off your rose-coloured glasses where Diane Westlake is concerned. She's no friend of mine."

She was shocked. "Trish?"

"Yes, God help me, I didn't believe her. But I believe Angie, Thelma, and I will not allow Diane to do any more damage to me and mine. Her malicious mischief-making ends here. Can I trust you to stay with Angie and look after her while I take care of this business?"

It jolted his aunt into vigorous loyalty. "Of course you can, Taylor. I won't leave her for a second." She stepped over to gently squeeze Angie's shoulder, a gruff and genuine appeal in her voice as she begged, "Please forgive me, my dear. I've been so very, very wrong."

Angie wearily lifted her head. "You were coming from a different place, Thelma. That's all. It's not your fault."

"Dad…"

Hamish was back with the three men Taylor trusted to get the job done. He held up his hand for them to wait then gently cupped Angie's face, drawing her gaze to his, wanting her to see, to know and trust his strength of purpose, his resolve to keep her safe. He tenderly stroked the tear stains from her cheeks as he spoke with all the latent force of his will.

"One hour at most, Angie, and I'll have Slater out of your life again and he'll have no taste for returning. That, I promise you."

She looked agonisingly unsure. "He's with Diane. We're invited to lunch with Adam. And *them*." Her mouth twisted in a travesty of a smile. "To make a meal of me, I guess."

"No. I'll be doing the serving, Angie." The violence he felt toward Slater could barely be contained, but Angie needed control from him. Iron control. "You stay here with Thelma. Don't move from this marquee until I return. Will you promise me to sit tight?"

Still the fear of everything going wrong—Slater sliding out of trouble—Diane backing him up. "Adam's our host, Taylor. And Brian has connections."

"Adam's my friend. He'll support me. And the outback has its own set of connections. It will be all right, believe me, Angie," he assured her, projecting the power he knew he could wield on this, his own ground. "I'll put some of my men on watch here so you'll feel protected. Okay?"

She bit her lip and nodded, too sick at heart to offer any more argument. She needed proof and Taylor needed action. He sat her down at a table in the back corner of the marquee and left her to Thelma's kindly fussing, knowing his aunt would do everything in her power to make amends for her faulty judgment.

A group of his jackeroos were standing just outside. He signalled Hamish and the others to join him there. "Chris..." he addressed the lad who always glowed under a smile from Angie. "There's a nasty city guy who's intent on making Angie's life miserable. Hamish will stay with you and point him out if he comes this way. You guys keep a watch out, will you, while I straighten this out with Adam Westlake?''

''I'll punch his lights out if he comes anywhere near,'' Chris growled.

Satisfied Angie was well guarded, Taylor proceeded to the Westlake marquee, outlining his plan to his three trusty lieutenants and what he required of each of them…Bill's bull strength and army training to intimidate, Joe's canny ability to see any attack or escape coming and foil it, Gary to fly the plane. Staunch support was readily given. They took up a stand by the bar in the hospitality marquee as Taylor made his way to the table where Adam was hosting a group of guests for lunch.

He had no difficulty picking out Brian Slater. Whatever other city guests had arrived were obviously being entertained elsewhere. Apart from Adam, Diane and her *city boyfriend,* there were three other station owners and their wives—all well-known to Taylor—and two empty chairs, presumably for him and Angie and predictably placed opposite Diane and Slater.

Adam saw him coming and hailed him heartily. ''Taylor, at last. We've been waiting for you. Where's Angie?''

''Don't tell me she's not with you,'' Diane chided prettily. ''I asked her especially.''

''Yes. Angie told me how well you planned the invitation, Diane,'' he stated coldly, icy blue eyes slicing through her deceit. He gripped the back of the chair designated for him and remained pointedly standing as he addressed his old friend. ''I'm sorry, Adam. I will not sit down with the man your daughter has brought here.

Nor will I suffer his presence in any company close to me. I am holding this chair to stop myself from tearing him apart here and now."

It stopped the buzz of bonhomie dead. Eyes turned from him to Slater in an appalled silence. Brian Slater's sangfroid was almost admirable, except Taylor felt the sliminess of it, just as Hamish had. The glossy handsome city slicker relaxed back in his chair, a quirky half-smile on his face as though prepared to be amused by Taylor's making an utter fool of himself.

Superficially he was quite a star, tanned and lean and dressed with casual elegance in designer country wear. His black hair was styled long enough to provide a romantic frame of waves and curls for finely sculpted features. His dark eyes gleamed with sharply intelligent calculation. The onus of proof was on Taylor and the sense that Slater was used to winning—confident of it— oozed from him. It made Taylor's skin crawl as he finally appreciated what Angie had been up against.

"Good God, man!" Adam expostulated. "What's he done?"

Taylor eyed Slater with contempt. "He's a spoilt to the bone, rich city kid, riding the fast lane, snorting cocaine, and believing he can have anything he wants, never mind the rights of others."

Slater's smooth brow wrinkled in mock bewilderment. "This is quite outrageous." His voice was calm, aimed at soothing ruffled feathers. "I've never even met you until this minute."

"You're also a psychopathic liar," Taylor declared with steely conviction. "Angie has given me chapter and verse on you, Slater."

"Oh, Angie." He waved a weary dismissal. "Diane will tell you I was nothing but polite to her. To me,

Angie Cordell was just a chick I lived with for a while…''

First mistake. Angie had won a lot of liking and respect amongst the station folk this week. There was a subtle stiffening around the table as Slater continued referring to her with an insulting edge of contempt.

''She took it hard when I dumped her. I thought she'd be over it by now. I tried to be friendly…''

''Like continually invading her life after she'd walked out of the relationship with you, having suffered too much of your abuse to ever want to be with you again,'' Taylor mocked savagely. ''Like filling her with dread at what you'd do next as you stalked her, month after month, ignoring her rejections, overriding her objections, laying siege to her apartment.''

Slater rolled his eyes in a show of pained disbelief. ''Angie told you that?'' He shook his head and sighed. ''I shall really have to consider suing her for slander if she goes on blackening my character like this. I assure you, the woman must be unstable…''

Second mistake. No one who'd met Angie would consider her unstable.

''Taylor, Brian comes from a highly reputable family,'' Diane put in with a touching air of wounded pride.

''A family who's been shovelling his sins under the carpet for years. Not to mention paying them off,'' he lashed at her.

''You only have Angie's word for all this,'' she defended.

''You're wrong, Diane. You told him Angie would be here, didn't you?''

She hesitated, faced with his absolute certainty.

''Her name might have come up. I talked about many of the people who'd be here.''

"All of them strangers to Slater except Angie. You must have had quite a conversation about her."

"Well, it was a coincidence, Brian's knowing her," she defended, realising vagueness wasn't going to work.

"And your meeting him—the one man who'd plagued her life and sanity—and bringing him here to do it again…that a coincidence, too, Diane?"

"I don't know what you're implying," she blustered.

"Better drop it, Diane. Drop it all," he warned bitingly. "Because I'm a witness to what Slater did to Angie, and I don't imagine anyone here thinks I'm unstable."

"A witness!" Slater squawked incredulously. "That's totally impossible. There was nothing to witness."

Taylor stared right through his charade of innocence. "I called Angie about the governess job the night you caught her alone and vulnerable. I was the man on the other end of the phone line when Angie used me as a bluff to get you out of her apartment. Which you'd entered by stealing her spare key and using it, despite her repeated refusals to see you again. Home invasion it's called, Slater. Violation of her rights."

"She obviously made up that story," he scoffed.

"Because of her rather obscure cry for help on the phone, I came to her apartment that night, Slater. At first she pretended she wasn't in. When I indentified myself, she hauled me inside in a frenzy of fear, then literally collapsed in a nervous heap, speechless, completely traumatised because you were still outside waiting for her, waiting to pounce again once you were confident of an all clear."

"This is a totally distorted interpretation of…"

"I saw you out there, Slater. I watched you waiting

to do what you wanted, to take more and more from Angie.''

He sneered. "You're repeating what *she* fed you and it's not the truth.''

Taylor's fingernails dug into the wooden frame of the chair. His hands itched to close around Slater's neck and squeeze the truth out of him. Nevertheless, he knew his best course was to keep ramming it down his throat. And convincing everyone else of it.

"You can't talk your way out of this one, Slater. I was there. I saw the state Angie was in. No one could play-act that. I was the one who calmed her down and gave her an escape from you, the one who phoned the police to move you on so I could remove her as cleanly as possible from your victimisation.''

"There is a very simple explanation for my presence there that night," he drawled with strained patience.

"Yes," Taylor agreed. "Angie had no family to help her, the women she shared the apartment with were away, and she had no one to turn to because the general run of people run scared of standing up to a wealthy, well-connected psychopath like you, and you thought you could get away with what you were doing.''

The oily scum leaned forward in reasoning appeal. "I tell you, she is hopelessly neurotic about our relationship.''

"You don't have a relationship with her anymore, Slater. And Angie has gained a family. Everyone on Giralang is her family. In fact, she now belongs to the whole outback family, none of whom gives a damn about your influential city connections. So you have nowhere to move except out of here with no return ticket. You came to hurt one of our own, to show her there was no escape from you.''

"Oh, this is absurd!" he cried, openly vexed now, glancing around for support.

There was none. Even Diane had turned her face away, wise enough to recognise which side her bread was buttered.

Taylor held up his hand to signal his men forward. He turned to Adam who sat stony-faced, deeply disgusted at having been deceived in Diane's special guest. "Mind if we borrow the Jeep outside, Adam? It will make a quick trip to the airstrip and Gary will fly Slater out if you have no objection."

"Key's in the ignition," he said in strong affirmation of Taylor's arrangements.

Gary, Joe and Bill moved around to crowd Slater's chair. He looked at them as though he couldn't believe what was happening.

"You have no right…" he began blustering.

"You're the one who has no rights here," Taylor corrected him.

No one raised a murmur of protest on his behalf. He glared at Diane. "You said these people were civilised."

"Provided *you're* civilised," Taylor said pointedly, "my men will give you courteous escort onto a flight from Mount Isa to Brisbane."

Slater rose to his feet, adopting an air of outraged dignity. "You and that deranged woman will be hearing from my solicitor."

"Make one more move against Angie and I will personally feed you to a crocodile," Taylor bit out, the violence he'd restrained shimmering with unmistakable intent. "Don't ever make the mistake of thinking I'll fight to your rules and rights, Slater. Out here we have our own. And the first rule is survival. We shoot mad beasts. We shoot diseased ones. I happen to feel a bullet is too clean for you.''

''You're talking murder, man.'' There was a very satisfying catch of fear in Slater's voice. He looked wildly around the table. ''In front of witnesses, too.''

''Didn't hear a thing,'' Adam declared.

''Taylor's talking about cattle, Adam,'' one of the other station owners blandly informed him.

''Yeah...culling trouble,'' another affirmed.

''Got to shoot venomous snakes,'' one of the wives remarked. ''Did it myself the other day.''

The line of support was unquestionable. Taylor gave it a moment to sink in then smiled his own satisfaction. It was a smile that promised deadly attrition.

''I'd strongly advise you never to step foot in the gulf country again, Slater. It's not unknown for city people to be taken by crocodiles. Through their ignorance of survival rules.''

He nodded to Bill who immediately took over. ''If you'll come this way, sir, we shall facilitate your departure.'' It was said with the military aplomb he'd never lost.

Slater glared at him, measured the beefy arms and shoulders of the men's cook, and decided to effect an exit on his own two feet. ''I have belongings in my tent,'' he stated angrily.

''We'll collect them on the way,'' Joe said with an obliging air.

There were no farewells. As the escort moved their responsibility out of the marquee, Taylor started to follow, wanting to check there was no last-minute resistance from Slater.

Adam's chair scraped back. ''I'll see him off, too,'' he said gruffly. He stood up and paused, frowning at his daughter. "Bad judgment, Diane. Don't be taken in so damned easily in future."

"I'm sorry, Dad," she said meekly, eyes cast down, a flush of shame—or suppressed fury—burning her cheeks. "He really fooled me."

"Better sort yourself out, girl," Adam admonished, "and put this behind you."

She nodded in humble submission.

Taylor wondered if the lowered lids veiled her frustration with the outcome of this last piece of malice, then dismissed the speculation as irrelevant. He'd pulled her fangs and delivered a warning she'd respect if she had any sense. Humiliation did not suit her. Besides which, Diane was first and foremost a survivor. Taylor was confident the warning would be heeded.

Adam clapped his shoulder as he joined him to see Slater loaded into the Jeep and taken away. "Got to thank you for that, Taylor. Wouldn't want my daughter any further involved with such a snake. Saved us a bundle of trouble, I reckon."

"He's poison all right," Taylor agreed, barely refraining from telling Adam his daughter was tarred with a similar brush, but hopefully, the shock of this dangerous misfire with Slater would serve as a sobering lesson to her, and no good would come of alienating a man who'd always been a staunch friend to him. Family invariably held first loyalty. Criticism of his daughter would not be welcomed. "Thanks for your ready support, Adam," he said warmly. "I appreciate it. And so will Angie."

"She all right?" he asked in quick concern.

"She will be." He nodded to the Jeep. "With him gone."

Gary was behind the wheel. Slater was jammed between Joe and Bill on the back seat and there was nothing smooth about him now. He looked as if he was in a hard place and sweating over it. Gary saluted Taylor, a silent assurance this business would be finished as arranged, then drove off on the first leg of returning Brian Slater to *his* family and connections who were more than welcome to him.

Taylor turned and offered his hand to Adam, "Thanks again, my friend."

"Pleasure." Adam's clasp was strong. "Mind you bring Angie to the dance tonight. We'll all make her feel at home."

Taylor nodded, hoping it would be true in a very deep sense, and Angie would always feel at home with him, his family and his friends. "I must get back to her now. Sorry about lunch."

Adam grinned. "Well, Diane might have to choke it down but you've given me a better appetite for it. Didn't like that city slicker even before you blasted him."

Satisfied their understanding was solid enough to hold their friendship together, Taylor took his leave, anxious to clear Angie's fears, then perhaps settle some of his own.

He wanted—needed—some time alone with her. It had been such a busy, crowded week. He'd meant to wait until they were back at Giralang before opening up on the issues burning in his heart but the double-barrelled encounter with Brian Slater had brought them to the surface in a searing rush. He knew what had driven Angie into his life. He had to know what had kept her in his arms.

And if she wanted to stay there for the rest of her life.

CHAPTER SEVENTEEN

TAYLOR had done it again. The wonder of it clung to Angie's mind, making the ride along the river bank a rosy haze. Her horse automatically followed his, picking their way toward a private picnic spot away from the camp. Taylor knew where he was going. She didn't care, as long as it was with him.

Occasionally she glanced at the sky, the amazing image of the plane flying Brian away vividly implanted in her memory. The blue expanse above, stretching from horizon to horizon, remained clear of any man-made object. Brian was gone. Never to return, Taylor had assured her.

Incredibly, they'd all taken her side—Taylor, Hamish, Thelma, everyone from Giralang, the friends she'd made throwing a protective ring around her, actively resolving her problem, the outback people standing firm in support of her, believing in her, caring about her, even Adam Westlake going so far as to castigate his daughter for her association with Brian. Never had she thought—nor imagined—this could happen to her.

It wouldn't have in the city. People simply didn't connect into a solid, all-encompassing network in an urban environment. This had to be something very special to the outback, and that something special had been given to her by the man riding beside her. Taylor Maguire. *He* had drawn her into his circle of belonging—the charmed circle—and she now belonged to it, too…one of them.

Angie marvelled at the turning point in her life that

had brought her to the man who answered everything for her. She remembered her first impressions; his aura of strength, the sense of endurance that defied anything to beat him, a man of action. All true, she thought, then quickly added compassion and caring. She doubted any other person would have come to her rescue as he had the night he'd called her in Brisbane. Then changing his mind about the job, for her sake. Now this...

Angie looked at him, her heart swelling with love.

He caught her gaze and smiled inquiringly. "Will here do?"

"Yes." Yes to anything with him, she thought.

They dismounted and tethered their horses to a log. Taylor laid a ground rug on a sandy stretch under the trees overhanging the river. The lunch-sized cool box Thelma had packed contained ham rolls, apples and cans of lemonade—simple fare but very welcome. The ride and the relief of being freed from Brian again had re-awakened Angie's appetite.

She and Taylor sat facing the soothing flow of water, munching away in a companionable silence. It wasn't until the food and drink were consumed that either of them felt like talking. Angie was content simply to be and Taylor appeared immersed in his own thoughts.

"Feeling better?" he finally asked, his clear blue eyes holding some inner tension as they scanned her face and took in her relaxed posture.

"On top of the world again," she assured him, a warm, tingly feeling spreading through her at his concern. "Thanks to you."

His mouth twisted self-mockingly. "It was as much for myself as it was for you, Angie. I want you to be happy here because I want you to stay with me. Which, in a very personal sense, makes me little different to Slater.''

"No! You're not like him at all," Angie protested. "Believe me, I know."

He shook his head. "I don't want to let you go, either. I understand his compulsion to keep you. I doubt there'll ever be another woman to match what you give me and I'll always be grateful for having known you…however briefly…in the span of my life."

Fear fluttered through her heart. Was he about to say her time with him was up? But why? What had she done wrong?

"You must have thought of Giralang as a safe place," he went on, his eyes searching hers, watching intently for the reflection of the truths he believed he was speaking. "I think you embraced the life there because it was one life you could have with relative peace of mind."

Her brain raced, clutching at other reasons she could put to him, anything to stave off the decision she felt coming. He paused and it took an effort of will not to rush in with argument, to wait and hear more of what he was thinking. To her intense relief, her silence prompted him to expand on how he saw her situation.

"Now I've made it even safer. Perhaps more attractive because of it. But it's not the only safe place in the world for you, Angie. I know Slater has stirred bad memories again." There was a flash of contempt in his eyes as he added, "but I doubt he'll be moving away from the protection of his connections in Brisbane for a long time to come."

She didn't doubt it, either. Brian would have been shaken to the core to find himself unsupported and totally isolated amongst a crowd of hostile people.

"Adelaide is a nice city. So is Perth," Taylor suggested quietly. "I'm sure they'd be every bit as safe as the outback. And I've seen how quickly you can adapt, Angie. You could make a new life for yourself in either place."

Her heart sank. It was the city prejudice again. Though perhaps it was less a prejudice than a worry about the future. It wasn't only her future at stake here, but his and Hamish's, as well. If the tie between them was to be broken, his reasoning obviously pointed to its being better done before expectations deepened. Hamish already wanted to hang on to her. And Taylor?

He sat with his knees up, forearms resting on them, hands linked between them, not reaching out to her with touch. He looked relaxed but she could feel the restraint he was imposing on himself, the determination not to use physical persuasion in this decision-making. Yet there was an aching appeal in the eyes holding hers.

"I need to know where you really want to be, Angie," he said bluntly. "I need a sense of direction from you. And it must be an honest one. You do see that, don't you?"

"Yes," she whispered, her throat constricting with an emotional awareness of how much depended on her reply.

Her initial fear was baseless. Taylor didn't want her to go. He just didn't feel it was fair to press her to stay if it wasn't truly right for her, so he was clearing the way for her to choose. With Brian's effect on her fresh on his mind, Taylor could not—would not—go down the same path, however much he wanted to keep her with him.

But how to convince him there wasn't any question in *her* mind? Angie was acutely conscious of this being another turning point, the most critical one of her life because what she most wanted was hanging on it. She was almost frightened to begin. Tension coursed through her, squeezing her heart into pounding painfully. There seemed no other course but to risk everything now. He'd asked for honesty. Angie knew she needed it, too.

"Do you love me, Taylor?"

The vulnerable yearning in her eyes seemed to be reflected in his.

"Yes," he answered simply.

"And I love you," she replied with soul-deep fervour. "You don't think it's enough to hold us together?"

Anguished uncertainty looked back at her. "I don't know, Angie. My life…everything I've lived for…is tied up with Giralang. I can't take it out of me. Not for anyone. I'm asking…can it be…is it…more than a safe place to you?"

Angie knew a straighforward, "Yes," would not suffice. Taylor's doubts went too deep to be easily erased. She had to make him understand why the truth was the truth before he would fully accept it.

"It's good to feel safe," she answered slowly. "It's good to be free of the shackles of fear because it allows you to see what's around you and get it in a perspective that isn't distorted. You remember the interview at the Hilton?"

He nodded.

"I told you then I wasn't looking to others to make something of my life for me. I needed time for myself."

"Healing time," he murmured.

"No. More than that. Time to sort out what had real meaning to me. What was important to my life. Apart from being free of Brian."

He pondered her words for several moments before

asking, "Have you come up with any answers that satisfy you?"

She smiled. "All of them, I think."

His responding smile was less sure. It appealed for her confidence. "I'd like to hear them."

She took a deep breath. "It might not be easy for you to relate to. Our backgrounds are very different, Taylor."

"Try me," he encouraged.

Somehow she had to *make* him understand. He probably wouldn't believe her answers otherwise. She averted her gaze, desperate to appear in control of herself. On impulse she leaned forward and picked up a handful of the sandy red earth around them and used it as a focus for Taylor's attention.

"See how this isn't packed solid? It trickles through my fingers, nothing holding it together. That's what my life felt like before I came to Giralang. Not just with Brian. All of it since my dad died. He was shot, trying to foil a robbery in a bank. I lost everything then."

"Surely your mother…"

"Mum couldn't hold herself together. She needed someone to lean on. She drifted through a string of boyfriends who took up most of her time. I became what's called a latch-key kid, more or less looking after myself."

She shot him a derisive look. "You think of the city as a place of entertainment, full of people to provide it. To me, it's rarely been anything but lonely. I think cities are the loneliest places in the world. No one has the time to get to know you as they do out here. They don't really want to know and they don't really care about you."

She heard the passion rising in her voice as she pleaded, "Do you think I want to go back to that when I've felt the kind of community life you have out here?

The caring and the sharing? The looking after each other?''

He frowned, seriously assessing her point. ''Some people can find it claustrophobic after a while, Angie, everyone knowing each other's business.''

He was thinking of Trish again! Angie had to swallow a surge of bitter resentment for the woman who had blighted his life and left a legacy of shadows that had to be fought. The anger of being misjudged shook her voice as she cried out against it.

''I craved the blanket of acceptance you call claustrophobic. I went looking for it while my mother sought the kind of love she wanted. The friends I had from conventional families weren't allowed out at night so I found other friends from similar situations to my own. I ran wild for years, looking for what you've had all your life...a place to be...with people who shared it...even though it was a life I hated!''

It moved him. He gestured an apology, his expression pained by her pain. ''Angie, I'm sorry. You needn't dig up these memories for me. If you're sure this life is what you want...''

''But *you're* not sure and I can't bear your doubting me,'' she protested, her heart aching with the need for his belief. ''It'll go on if you don't hear me now. If you don't understand...''

''Then tell me,'' he invited softly, caringly.

Tears blurred her ears. She fiercely blinked them back, swallowed hard, and forced herself on. ''By the time I was fourteen I'd joined up with a local gang led by a guy called Trav Logan. There was a kind of sympathy between us. We clicked. He watched out for me and kept me out of the bad stuff. But he had a record of trouble with the police and when the guys in the gang raided a warehouse of electrical goods he got caught. So I lost him, too. But at least something good happened to him. The judge gave him a choice of six months on an outback station—it was a special program—or time in a correctional institution.''

"So he was your friend who found what he wanted in the outback," Taylor murmured, remembering what she'd told him all those months ago.

"Yes," she replied quickly, relieved he had listened to her then and was trying to put it together now. "Having come here myself, I understand why he felt what he did about it," she pressed earnestly. "It's much bigger than the city and life takes on a different scale. It has a vast, intricate pattern to it with challenges that have to be met, yet there's the sense it's never going to change on you. The pattern will stay the same, no matter what.''

"And that's important to you?" Taylor gently probed.

"I think for both Trav and me, it's like the solid foundation that had eluded us until we experienced this. You were brought up with it so it's always been there for you, a constant you take for granted. We didn't have constants. The things in our lives kept shifting, even as we clung to what seemed like some kind of solidarity. A gang. A sometime mother…''

Taylor winced. ''I remember you saying your mother died when you were fourteen.''

The anguish of that terrible time flooded out of her memory and she jerked her gaze away from his, staring blindly at the river for several moments as she struggled for calm. The flow of the water soothed her inner agitation and gradually caught her attention. It moved endlessly in one direction. There never was a backward flow, she reflected. None with death, either.

She *had* to move forward, giving Taylor the direction

he needed, the understanding of where she'd come from
so he could go forward with her. No looking back. No
going back. They could make a future together if he
would only put the past to rest.

With regathered resolution, she explained, "Mum had
gone to a party where they smoked marijuana. About
two o'clock in the morning, she went pillion-riding on
a motorbike. It crashed at high speed and she was
killed."

Her flat recitation produced a heavy silence, loaded
with the emptiness left by her mother's death. Her own
bleak sadness was echoed in Taylor's voice when he
finally remarked, "I guess that removed your last bit of
security."

She turned to him on a fierce roll of emotion. "I hate
drugs. I hate what they do to people. I like it that we're
free of all that out here. And the air is clean. You see
all the stars at night. You don't know how lucky you
are, Taylor. Whatever struggles you have are *with* nature, not against it."

"I see what you mean, Angie," he said comfortingly.
"It always feels good to leave the city pollution behind
and…"

"No. It's more than that. Much more," she cried.
"There's the belonging, Taylor. You don't know how
wonderful it is to belong. To really feel it after not having it. When Mum died, my aunt—Dad's older sister—
took me in, doing her moral duty with an iron fist in a
respectable glove. There was no love dispensed. Only
discipline. And once I was through teacher's college and
had a teaching post, she couldn't wash her hands of me
fast enough."

"She told you unequivocally there was no going back

to her?'' he questioned, horrified that any family member would be so ruthless in dispossessing her.

Angie grimaced at the truth he found so unpalatable. But truth was truth. ''Not for anything,'' she told him flatly. ''She made that clear. Though God knows I earned my keep with her. If she'd only shown…just a little affection.''

The realisation of her aloneness was starkly visual in his eyes. At least he understood that much now. Angie heaved a desolate sigh and tried to explain more.

''I swear I did my best to fit in, Taylor. She was a spinster, very much set in her own ways. It just wasn't right for her or for me.'' She pleaded another difficult truth. ''Any more than it was right with Brian, though I fooled myself into believing it could be. I think I was starved for someone to love me. I kept on trying to make the connection with him work until I realised it never would.''

Taylor startled her by reaching over and taking her hand, interweaving her fingers with his. The intensity in his eyes caused her heart to catapult around her chest. ''Does our connection work, Angie?'' he asked softly. ''Or are you trying hard again?''

''I never had to try,'' she answered, her nerves almost unbearably strained by the desperate desire to convince him. ''I felt the connection from the beginning. When the interview for the governess ended, I didn't want to leave you. It wasn't because of Brian. It was *you*, Taylor. I felt instinctively you had what I needed. Then later, that night, I never had a doubt about going with you. The trust was automatically there. The trust and the overwhelming wish, simply to be with you.''

''You had the same pull on me, Angie, though I tried to deny it,'' he said ruefully.

"Because I was a city woman?"

"Yes. Though I realise now you didn't belong any-where. You hadn't yet found a place to call home."

Tears pricked her eyes at his understanding. "You are the place, Taylor. You and Giralang are one. To love you is to love what made you what you are. I've found my home..." The tears welled and spilled "...If you love me," she finished huskily.

"Love you..." He moved so fast, Angie was caught breathless as he lowered her to the rug and leaned over her, tenderly trapping her beneath him, his eyes elo-quently begging her forgiveness for his doubts. "You've just saved me from the hell of imagining a life without you. I love you so much, Angie, it was killing me to even consider you might want to leave."

"Oh, Taylor..." More tears welled. "I would die in-side without you."

"Don't cry, my darling." He frantically kissed the wet streaks from her eyes. "I can't bear for you to feel hurt."

She wound her arms around his neck. "Just love me. Love me and all the hurt will go away."

"Angie..." It was the warm breath of love, caressing her skin, seeping into her heart. His kiss said it more truly, pouring all the passion of his feeling through her, the loving and cherishing and yearning to be one with her. "Angie...will you marry me? Have children with me?"

"Yes..." She held him tight, revelling in the power and strength of him, the stability and solidity he offered her, promised her, gave her. "Yes, Taylor, yes!"

No past...only the future...a future together stretching forward to span the rest of their lives...and the promise of it...the commitment to it...throbbed through the heat of the afternoon as they made love to each other on the bank of a river that kept flowing onward, a force of nature feeding its life-giving water to the timeless land of the outback.

Hamish grinned as he watched his father and Angie circling the dance floor, their solo waltz clapped by everyone who'd come to the picnic races. Angie looked real pretty in her red dress and his dad was whirling her around, both of them laughing like they were bubbling with happiness.

"You said your dad was never going to get married again," Jessie complained, put out because she'd had no warning of the announcement that had just been made.

Hamish, who had been hugging the secret for hours, turned a smug face to her. "*You* said he was going to marry Diane Westlake."

Jessie huffed. "Well, he *is* going to get married anyhow."

"He's got to so everything will be right," Hamish informed her cheerfully. "Angie said we're going to have a big family so there'll always be Maguires at Giralang. I'll have a whole gang of brothers and sisters and they'll be looking up to me as the leader."

"You mean more kids?" Wayne frowned disapproval. "We'll be kicked off the computer to give them a turn, Hamish."

"Nah... Dad's got to keep updating computers. We'll put them on an old one to play with, Wayne."

"Yeah..." He grinned with relish. "We can show 'em a thing or two."

"*I'll* be watching," Jessie said archly.

Wayne gave her a dark look. "Better tell Angie you

only want brothers, Hamish. Girls just want to mess up everything.''

''Angie doesn't mess up,'' Hamish pointed out.

''Yeah, well, she's different.''

Different…she sure was, Hamish thought, watching his father and Angie dancing together. She'd made a big difference to everything. And it was good seeing her so happy with his dad. Her eyes were all sparkly, like she had stars in them.

He wondered if she knew what Giralang meant. It was something he could tell her now she was going to stay forever. She'd like knowing it was an old Aboriginal word from a long time ago, before even the first Maguire came to the gulf country. As far back as anyone could remember their home had been called Giralang.

It meant…the place of stars.

Always had been.

Always would be.

LOOK FOR OUR FOUR FABULOUS MEN!

Each month some of today's bestselling authors bring
four new fabulous men to Harlequin American Romance.
Whether they're rebel ranchers, millionaire power brokers
or sexy single dads, they're all gallant princes—and
they're all ready to sweep you into lighthearted fantasies
and contemporary fairy tales where anything is possible
and where all your dreams come true!

You don't even have to make a wish…
Harlequin American Romance will grant your every desire!

Look for Harlequin American Romance
wherever Harlequin books are sold!

HAR-GEN

HARLEQUIN PRESENTS®

HARLEQUIN PRESENTS
men you won't be able to resist
falling in love with...

HARLEQUIN PRESENTS
women who have feelings
just like your own...

HARLEQUIN PRESENTS
powerful passion in
exotic international settings...

HARLEQUIN PRESENTS
intense, dramatic stories that will keep you
turning to the very last page...

HARLEQUIN PRESENTS
The world's bestselling romance series!

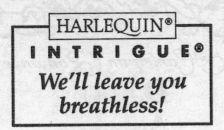

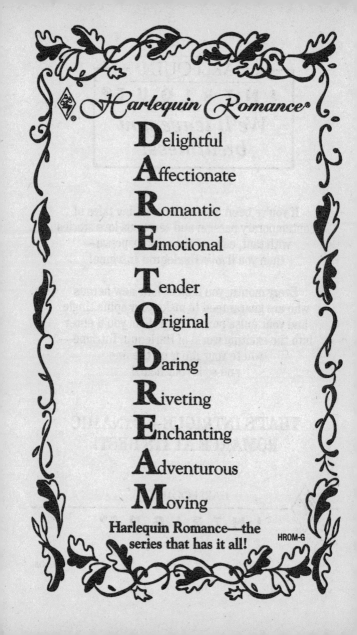

Harlequin Romance®

Delightful

Affectionate

Romantic

Emotional

Tender

Original

Daring

Riveting

Enchanting

Adventurous

Moving

Harlequin Romance—the
series that has it all!

HROM-G

Harlequin® Historical

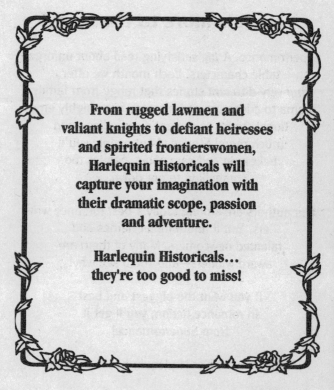

From rugged lawmen and
valiant knights to defiant heiresses
and spirited frontierswomen,
Harlequin Historicals will
capture your imagination with
their dramatic scope, passion
and adventure.

Harlequin Historicals...
they're too good to miss!